Song About Pity

Written by

Avigdor Dagan

English Translation by

Patrik Munzar

Mazo Publishers

Song about Pity

by Avigdor Dagan (Viktor Fischl)

ISBN 978-1-956381-450

Translated from Czech to English
by Patrik Munzar
patrik.munzar@gmail.com

Originally published in Czech, 1982 – Píseň o lítosti

Mazo Publishers
Website: www.mazopublishers.com
Email: info@mazopublishers.com

54321

Through this book, the author has created a literary memorial for the perished Skalica, Czechoslovakia Jewish community.

At the Yad Vashem Holocaust Remembrance Center in Jerusalem, the list of people killed during the Holocaust from Skalica includes the last names of most of the protagonists in the book (Sefranek, Timfeld, Braun, Weiss, Klein, Beinhacker, Kohut, Fischer, and Tolnai).

Contents

About the Author

Avigdor Dagan (1912-2006), originally named Viktor Fischl, was a prolific Czech Israeli author and politician. He was born in Hradec Králové, Čechy, Austria-Hungary (now Czech Republic). He died in Jerusalem, Israel. At the beginning of World War II, he escaped from occupied Czechoslovakia to the United Kingdom. He served as an associate to the Czech exile Foreign Secretary of State, Jan Masaryk, in London. After the war, he returned to his homeland but emigrated to Israel in 1949 and, at that time, changed his name from Viktor Fischl to Avigdor Dagan. He then served as an Israeli ambassador to Austria, Norway, Poland, and other countries until his retirement.

Before and during the war, the author wrote mainly poetry but later focused on collections of short stories and novels, which became very popular. His most famous work, *The Court Jesters*, was translated into at least 12 languages. The novel *Song about Pity* was originally written in 1948, but could not be published due to the communist coup in Czechoslovakia. A Hebrew translation appeared in 1951, but the Czech original was published for the first time in 1982 by a Czech exile publisher in Canada, and at that time, a prologue and an epilogue were added.

About the Translator

Patrik Munzar (*1969) is a Stanford-trained physician and publicist, originally from the Czech Republic. He works as a psychiatrist in Northern California, where he lives with his wife Miriam and their 13 children. He would like to acknowledge his daughters Abigail and Rachel and his son Raphael for their help with editing the manuscript.

The translator met the author, Avigdor Dagan, when he was signing the Czech edition of the book when it was re-published in 1992 in the Czech Republic. At that time, he shared with the translator that he got the inspiration for this story from his own childhood memories. Both his maternal and paternal grandparents lived close to each other in small towns named Skalica and Holíč – those towns are in Slovakia now, but just next to the Czech border (the river described in the novel is the river Morava which creates the border between the Czech Republic and Slovakia). He spent most of his summers with them, and his grandfathers were real characters depicted in the novel (but he changed their last names).

ca 1930s Czechoslovakia
in the provincial towns of Skalica and Holíč

Prologue

It was not easy to estimate the age of the good-looking man in the gray suit of unusual style who had just gotten out of the midday train from Břeclav and who was inspecting the empty platform, as if he wanted to make sure that it was really the station to which he had intended to arrive. His oval, sun-tanned face with dark, widely opened eyes was young, almost conspicuously young, compared with his thick and clearly not-fully-manageable hair interwoven with silver, with his lowered shoulders, and above all with his almost feeble gait. Upon first glance, it was difficult to tell if he was an old man with a young face or a young fellow who had been run down by a long and arduous journey.

Dispatcher Tomík was unable to decide. For a moment, he felt that he knew that face from somewhere, but for the living God – as his mother would say – was not sure where to place it. One thing was, however, clear. The stranger planned to remain here only for a short time. Apparently, he did not intend to stay – he arrived with just one piece of luggage – a small briefcase, like one used in the past by traveling salesmen for their samples. One of those salesmen, Kantůrek, used to live here, recalled dispatcher Tomík, but traveling salesmen completed their travels a long time ago.

God knows – (as we are still saying even though we should not) – where he came from and whom he wanted to visit. However, when he looked around the platform, he immediately knew where to exit the railway station and did not ask for any advice, and that was the only thing that was raising doubts if he was indeed a stranger. Perhaps he should call and report it to the authorities, but he had other worries now. The train from Břeclav delivered a lot of mail packages, and it was necessary to record everything. Additionally, a local train from Veselí will be here soon, and the comrade station superintendent was again sitting at some meeting, and Tomík was alone for all the work. He shrugged his shoulders and continued with all his assignments.

Meanwhile, the man who a few minutes ago had exited the train walked on the road leading from the station to the town center. The noon sun was blazing, and the white dust that was swirling by his somewhat shuffling gait was rising up and then again coming down on the road so that the footprints were almost disappearing without a trace.

Also, at that time, when they were taking them away to the transport, they used this route, even though in the opposite direction, from the town square where they gathered them to the railway station where they packed them into the freight cars. But even then, he remembered, the clouds of white dust were rising up under their steps and again fell down to cover their traces.

He was unable to tell why he had arrived. He knew about what he would find, but mainly about what he would not find. He knew that he would return torn up, as if he had worked his way through a dense thicket of thorns. He had postponed this trip for a long time. But he knew that he had to take this journey one day.

Before he reached the town square, he knew that the place he returned to differed from the one he had left. Even though the small stores he remembered from the past were still there, he did not find the names of the original owners or their heirs; there were mostly only signs with the new, laughably composed names of various cooperatives and nationalized businesses. Linguistic spoils marked not only Aaron Timfeld's sawmill but also Spitzer's bakery and a little basket- and brush-making store that used to belong to old Abeš Tolnai.

Upon reaching the town square, he saw that the same had happened to Kahan's tinsmith's workshop, to Šefránek's tailor's store, to Samuel Klein's drapery and fabric retail, as well as to Beinhacker's butchery, in front of which now gathered a group of women with empty bags, patiently waiting in line for their turn.

The town square, with its pavement hot from the noontime sunlight, appeared otherwise deserted. But Daniel saw himself in the middle of the crowd. They were standing over there where the shade formed by the church's tower split the market's rectangular plan.

Rounded up and arranged by families with all the belongings left to them, packed in briefcases and luggage, hastily tied with belts and twines, they were surrounded by men in black uniforms with carbines on their shoulders and dogs on chains.

Nearby, next to the houses, stood farmers and their wives who watched, apparently feeling somewhat uncomfortable, how the families were lined up into fours and were shoved by the butts of the soldiers' rifles who urged them to move faster.

Once in a while, some women bit their fingers, and one peasant crumpled his hat between his palms in bewilderment, but most of them just stood there and looked ahead with apathy. But there were also those who were not hiding their joy from what was happening in front of their eyes.

Even now, they were making various jokes and seemed happy that they could loudly and openly voice what in the past they were only brave enough to tell behind the backs of those who stood there as a fearful flock, rounded up by cracking whips and dogs showing their teeth. Only limping Kate, who used to work as their maid, did not hide her tears.

He could name all of them, row after row. Even today, after everything which separated him from that day so many years ago, he remembered who was standing with whom, who was supporting whom, and who was trying to calm whom down.

Rabbi Kupfer, taller than the others, stood in the first row with his quiet wife, who was even at this moment removing specks of dirt from his dark coat without saying a word. His full black beard gave his face even more dignity than before as he looked somewhere high above the houses surrounding the square. Next to him, *Rosh Hakol* Aaron Timfeld, who was hunched under the weight of his luggage as well as under the burden of foreboding for their future, was also lowering his eyes down. Behind them, the butcher Beinhacker was touching with his massive hand again and again his vest where the golden chain he had liked to play with used to hang in the past, but not anymore. And with a glare at Timfeld, he repeated pretty loudly so that everybody could hear him: "This is how far we have ended up!" And after a few moments again: "We have really achieved something." But nobody paid attention to him; each of them had his own worries. Only the retired teacher Lebenhart repeatedly said: "This is unheard of, unheard of." Even that, however, sounded as if he was only repeating it mechanically while thinking about something else.

Grandfather Gabriel Menasse stood at the head of several rows in which were gathered the families of his sons Jacob, Moshe, and Ruben, along with all of Daniel's aunts and cousins. Daniel now saw himself as he removed the glasses from the tearful eyes of his cousin David and wiped them with the edge of his scarf, which had been wrapped around his neck by his mother. Aunt Rebecca, pregnant again, and Uncle Jacob – his favorite out of all his uncles – supported her. On her other side stood Grandmother Theresa, with her hands ready to help, as always, although she was now even smaller than usual, and it seemed that she herself needed somebody to lean on. Theresa's second daughter-in-law, the widow of her youngest son, Daniel's father, was also here. She was the daughter of Philip Taub, who stood next to Gabriel. Daniel recalled how Grandfather Gabriel and Grandpa Philip argued, as always, whether God was strict and just, or merciful and full of compassion.

"He is punishing us," said Grandfather Gabriel. "He is punishing us because we have sinned." After a moment, however, while looking at the men with carbines and people standing behind them, he added: "Even their time will come. He will punish them too. They are sinning more than we have ever sinned, and God is just."

And Grandpa Philip, who had been just listening for a long time, shrugged his shoulders and finally said: "He punishes but also forgives. God knows what he is doing. We all are in his hands."

At that very moment, similarly as then, the bell from the church tower rang and struck noon. Everything which had been before his eyes just a few minutes ago suddenly disappeared. Only the women standing in line in front of the butcher shop where Beinhacker used to rule were still there.

Daniel woke up to reality. He only just recalled how Grandpa Philip added: "We survived so much. He will help us to survive even this." And he said to himself: "Only I. From all of them, only I survived." He passed his hand over his eyes as if he was trying to dispel a bad dream and resumed his walk with brisk steps.

He initially wanted to walk through the entire town before returning to where he had lived as a child. At the lower end of the square, in the second house from the corner which used to belong to Grandfather Gabriel, lived Gabaňa, supervisor of the cooperative malting house. Daniel wanted to enter the roughly paved courtyard where the barley used to be stored and where it was possible to plunge your hand into the warm grain and let it shed from your palm back to the sack. He would have also liked to step into the large room where a large old armchair made from dark leather used to stand in the corner next to the window. Grandfather Gabriel used to spend much of his time there while reading the sacred books and smoking one of his many pipes that had lined the shelf on the wall behind the armchair. He, however, just peeped into the open gateway and saw there that they were loading sacks onto the truck and thus decided to walk away.

He then passed through the narrow street they used to cross with Grandpa Philip on their way to the synagogue. He was not sure whether it had any official name back then, but everybody had called it Windy Lane as it was always breezy there, and even during the warmest summer days, there was a cool shade there. Nowadays, however, everything had to be in order. He noticed the sign on the street corner, which indicated that the road was renamed Soviet Cosmonauts' Street. At the end of the road, he made a right turn into the oval opening of the white wall surrounding the courtyard. Above the entrance to the former synagogue, an inscription in large red letters announced that it was now the Yalta movie theater. He quickly left the place. For a moment, he had to lean on the trunk of the only tree in the street, in whose shade their dog Dak always used to wait for Grandfather Philip.

He then slowly walked through Creekside Street up to the hill called the Small Grove. It was there where both his grandfathers used to go for strolls, perpetually arguing about whether God was strict or lenient, just or merciful.

Once he reached the Small Grove, he was pretty tired and sat on the parched grass at the edge of the birchwood. He was also hungry and unpacked from his bag some food he had brought with him, just in case. Even after he ate, however, he still felt weak. He was unable to continue his journey at the moment. He tried to rise up but became dizzy, and his head was spinning. He thus sat down again. While leaning on a nearby birch, he stared ahead into space.

Then he closed his eyes.

Chapter 1

Ivanko

At half-past four in the morning, the shepherd Ivanko blew his horn while standing at the upper end of the street. The tall entry gates of the houses surrounding the unpaved road on both sides of the road opened as if on command. The mud of the street, which would dry up by noon under the July sun, was still soft. The entire road was still bedewed from the moisture of the night.

From the gates, they drove cattle to the pasture. From Tomík's house, two brindled cows marched out, from Vašica's, three white oxen with wide twisted horns with the ends pointing to the ground, from the opposite side of the road, from Gabaňa's, a young heifer. The long lowing of the cows, the squeaky hinges of the opening and closing gates, the pleading call of the cock's crowing, and the barking of Ivanko's dog named Gipsy, a black mongrel with a shaggy tail, combined with the sound of Ivanko's horn formed the unchangeable first chord of awakening day.

When he reached the other end of the street, Ivanko again raised the horn to his lips, and, as if under the spell of its call, more and more new gates opened up before him. The herd was already lining up on its own. The way was familiar to them. They knew that Ivanko would drive them up to the wagon road, across the wooden bridge above the dried-up riverbed, then around the fields and potato patches, and up to the meadows behind the Wet Grove.

With their swaying strides, the cows were slowly dragging ahead on the road. One could see the prominent ribs underneath their skin as the summer was dry. Since spring, it hardly rained twice, and when it did, the water scarcely softened the layer of dust and did not seep through the hardened crust of the parched earth. The weeping and cursing of the despairing farmers who were getting ready to plow in dried-up sprouts of grain did not help any more than pious Calvary processions praying for rain.

The shepherd looked up to heaven and shook his heavy head, covered with a hole-ridden and faded broad-brimmed hat. His weather-beaten face, forever covered with a stubbly beard, frowned. He thought of how muggy it would be again today and angrily hit the stone on the road with his knotted walking stick. Even though it was still early in the morning, the flies were already starting to attack the emaciated bodies of the cows, who swung their tails in vain. From time to time, some of the restless heads of the cattle left the line, and Gipsy gathered them back to the flock while loudly barking.

When Ivanko with the herd was already crossing the bridge over the dried-up riverbed, the entrance door to a yellow house opened. It was the house between the gate through which farmer Tomík's brindled cows recently walked and the portal from which Vašica's oxen wobbled out with heavy loftiness. And in the crack of light coming out of that door, the head of an about ten-year-old boy suddenly appeared. His black hair was unkempt, and his sun-burned oval face with wide-open dark eyes was unable to hide several speckled freckles on his rather wide and curious nose.

The boy looked carefully on both sides of the street before moving out his sun-tanned body on strong but barefooted legs, dressed only in short patched-up trousers of ambiguous color connected to two twine strings that served as suspenders. He crossed with certain secrecy the doorstep and quietly closed the door of the house behind him. He made several small and hesitating steps towards the upper end of the street, but then as if he had gathered some courage, he set off at a good pace while trying to pretend that there was nothing unusual in his early morning stroll. He soon, however, started to run while leaving behind him footprints in the dust, softened by the nighttime dew.

He stopped after crossing the wooden bridge once he saw in front of him Ivanko's herd, moving slowly up on the road between potato patches towards the Wet Grove. He was sure he would not lose the shepherd from his sight now. He jumped into the ditch which lined up the path, together with the dusted wildings. He then picked up a branch from the ground and walked through the dried-up ditch while carefully bowing down and pushing away the stinging nettles with his stick. When he drew near the herd, he stooped even more and continued on his journey. At times he was almost crawling.

The thought of Ivanko made children shudder. It was the scariest threat if your mother told you: "I do not know what to do with you. I will sell you to Ivanko!" or more simply: "Just wait – Ivanko will take you away!" Nobody really knew who had first identified Ivanko as the bogey man or why, but it was unnecessary to think it through as the threat was quite effective for years, and that was more or less its purpose. Children whispered that Ivanko ate dogs, stole newborns, and communed with the devil. The only thing people knew for sure about Ivanko was that he lived alone with his dog in the wooden shack on the hill above the vineyards where nobody else ever entered, that he daily drove the cattle to pastures behind the Wet Grove, that every evening he took his entrusted herd back down to the gates of the houses, that he never talked to anybody, that once per month he got really drunk in the Kohút's pub and then staggered to the center of the town square where he cursed loudly about some invisible rival while swinging around his whip till the bailiff Ferenčák took him to the town's jail where he slept till he sobered up, and next day early in the morning he again peacefully drove the cattle to the pastures.

That was all the children knew about Ivanko. But the fact that nobody knew anything more and nobody could find out anything else about him put together with their mothers' threats made the shepherd a mysterious and dreadful character in the children's minds. Some of them believed that the devil taught him to understand the language of animals, that his black dog was, in fact, a spellbound hell-dweller given to him by the demon himself as a servant, as Ivanko signed a pledge to him with his own blood, that the shepherd turned into a werewolf at night, and God knows what else. But however much they gave rein to their imagination, however much they tried to overtake each other in devising horrors attributable to Ivanko, they never lost the feeling that it was still not enough and that nobody had yet got to the root of the true secret of his dark aureole.

And it was just this secret that kept the unkempt black-haired head of the boy Daniel awake. He was crawling on his knees through the ditch next to the road while avoiding stinging nettles and while making sure that he would not lose sight of Ivanko, and that he himself would remain unseen. A large toad sitting on the ground of the dried-up ditch croaked piercingly just in front of Daniel's face. It frightened him, and he almost shouted. But he immediately returned to his senses, laid down, and remained completely motionless for a while. The dog started to bark but soon quieted down again, and Daniel silently slunk ahead.

Once the herd reached the Wet Grove, it had to curve around the corner of the forest. The boy ran like an arrow to the other side of the road and pressed himself to the trunk of a big tree. Then he jumped swiftly like a squirrel from tree to tree, hiding behind their enormous trunks and berating himself whenever his feet did not land on a patch of soft moss, and dry branches snapped under the weight of his strong legs as a result.

He passed the corner of the forest that way, and once he slunk to the trees on its edge, he saw Ivanko's herd, which had just reached the pastures. The cattle started to gnaw on short half-parched stalks of grass with their heavy heads bent deeply down to the ground. They took their time as they slowly spread over the slope while chewing on the lean pasture.

Daniel, hidden behind the giant oak tree at the edge of the forest, watched the shepherd. Ivanko stood for a few moments while leaning on his walking stick, but then gave a signal with his cane to the dog, which immediately started to bark and dashed away to round up a white heifer that went too far down on the slope. He then reached into the tattered bag hanging on his shoulder and took out something to eat. After that, he turned around and walked to the forest. The boy held his breath and pressed himself even closer to the tree trunk. But the shepherd changed direction and sat down among the forked roots of the tree at the corner of the forest from where he had a good view of the herd at the pasture. He was still, however, a stone's throw away from the boy.

He sat there while chewing something and looking around. The leaves hung vertically on the motionless branches of quieted trees, and the white pillows of the clouds stood calmly high in the sky. Once he finishes his meal, he will call the devil and will start to practice some sorcery, the boy thought, and his heart began to beat rapidly.

But Ivanko, once he finished chewing on the last crust, laid down on the ground, covered his face with his hole-ridden broad-brimmed hat, and fell asleep. Daniel could hear even from a distance his rattling breath. The boy felt somewhat disappointed but also relieved. He was disappointed that his quest for Ivanko's secret ended up with such a failure, but he also recalled Mother's words: "Whoever is too curious will age fast." He still had the opportunity to slink quietly from the forest to the road and then run back home. But he also recalled what his mother would say whenever he was late for the dinner, whenever he did not wash his hands, or whenever he did not want to go to bed: "Just wait – Ivanko will pick you up."

Grandfather Philip taught him that bogeymen were only in fairy tales and that there was no reason to fear anybody. Who should he believe? Ivanko is not in a fairy tale, he snores lying within a stone's throw of here, and he eats dogs and takes away misbehaving children. Mom herself said that. Who would not be scared of him?

About two or three steps away from Daniel, there was a shrub covered with blueberries. The boy, who had sneaked out of the house without breakfast, started to feel hungry. He decided to eat from the shrub while the shepherd was sleeping. However, what if Ivanko was just pretending to sleep? Maybe he knows that Daniel is following him. Perhaps he did not summon the devil up only because he was aware that Daniel was watching him. Maybe he was pretending to sleep so as to torture him longer. He knows that I am hungry. That is why he himself started to eat – to arouse Daniel's appetite. He knows that I am not brave enough to reach down for a blueberry so that I would not be noticed. But I will not give up as I have no fear, he tries to convince himself.

Grandfather says that I do not need to fear anybody. But it at once occurred to him that Grandfather had been saying something else. He had said: "A good man does not need to fear anybody." But he had also added: "Whoever fears God does not need to fear others." That is how it is. That is what Grandfather Philip says, and that is something different.

Am I a good person? I torment the cats and pull Dak's tail. I wander around with the other boys and come home late for dinner and bother Mom. And that time I beat my Cousin David because he did not want to play cops and robbers. And I put sharp pins on cantor Hercka's chair, stole sugar candies from Mom's store, picked eggs from the bird nests together with Jura Tomík and ... no, I am not a good man.

And I do not fear God enough either. Last year, during the big fast on Yom Kippur, I slipped out of the synagogue at noontime and ate half of the goose liver before coming back. Mom was surprised at how well I was tolerating the fast and suspected our limping maid, Kate. But I did not confess and left suspicion on her. No, I am not a good man. And that is why I have to fear.

Nevertheless, I am not afraid, he decided suddenly and made a step towards the blueberry shrub. But he immediately jumped back and pressed himself firmly to the tree, his heart throbbing almost in his neck. He could hear somebody's heavy strides on the road at the edge of the forest, and the shepherd's dog that was resting in the shade next to his master's body lifted his head up and straightened his ears. Then, from the place where the unknown walker stopped, a cuckoo call suddenly sounded:

"Cuckoo, cuckoo."

Barking, Gipsy rushed to the curve on the road. In a moment, the dog returned, wildly wagging its shaggy tail and jumping around the giant who was dressed as a vagabond in rags, but had a good-natured smile on his oval face. Daniel recognized him as old Karolek.

He was the local idiot, dirty and lousy, but tame and harmless. Nobody ever tried to scare the children with Karolek. They laughed at his feeble mind, the children followed him and mocked him, but Karolek always only answered with his bright smile and with the call of a cuckoo. People claimed that he fed on mice and frogs, and they loathe his lice. When they met, they scratched themselves from a distance instead of greeting him, but they never expelled him from the village as Karolek was also helpful. He was able to carry a calf on his shoulders, and whenever a wheel broke under a fully loaded rack wagon, they always called for Karolek to lift the carriage up and hold it by his back so that they could replace the wheel. As a reward, they gave him some booze, and the giant started to laugh loudly, and instead of thanks, he just made the call of a cuckoo.

He was now squatting in front of Ivanko's stretched-out body. The shepherd, woken up by Gipsy's barking, pushed the hole-ridden hat away from his cheek. He blinked but did not get up. Then, with the bright smile and a moony face of a simpleton, Karolek shouted out:

"Cuckoo, cuckoo."

"Go away, you devil!" snapped the shepherd at him and swung his cane around. But Karolek was still smiling and bluntly repeated:

"Cuckoo."

Then he poked into the deep pocket of his sackcloth pants, drew out the bottle, and gave it to Ivanko.

"Good."

Ivanko leaned on his elbow, grabbed the bottle, uncorked the plug with his teeth, and put the neck to his lips.

"Good?" asked the fool while watching him with his constant smile.

"Good. Cuckoo. Good. Cuckoo," rejoiced Karolek and he started to slap his thighs. He then poked again into his bottomless pocket and drew out a set of old, greasy, and worn-out cards.

"Good?" he asked while holding the cards in his hand.

"Good." The shepherd sat up and stretched.

"Good, cuckoo, good," the fool clapped and sat up noisily on the ground facing Ivanko.

Ivanko distributed cards into two identical piles. He then pointed his cane towards the clouds and divided the sky into halves by waving his stick. He waved to the right and said: "Mine." Then he waved to the left and said: "Yours."

Karolek made the call of a cuckoo showing his approval.

Ivanko played the card and drank from the bottle that sat between both players. Karolek flipped over his card and said:

"Good."

Then Ivanko again flipped over Karolek's card, and the fool continued to smile and said:

"Bad."

So there they were, placing card over card, and the tense silence was interrupted only by the buzzing of the flies and gadflies, by occasional mooing, and by Karolek's: "Good... Bad... Good... Bad."

The shepherd won the game and sipped from the fool's bottle. Then, he pointed with his cane at one of the clouds on Karolek's half of the sky and said: "Mine." Karolek again distributed the cards, and they continued to play. Ivanko drank from the bottle, and Karolek always shouted into the tense silence with the same: "Good... Good... Bad... Bad."

Nothing else was happening. How boring, thought the boy. He sat there behind the tree with his legs crossed and said to himself: So this is the big secret I was searching for.

The sun rose up, and the satiated cattle laid down on the hard ground and slowly waved their tails to repel gadflies. The booze from Karolek's bottle was disappearing down Ivanko's throat, and a prominent curved vein on his forehead became more visible.

Nothing else was happening. Grandfather Philip was right. There was nothing to fear.

The boy was becoming hungry and started to think with disappointment about how to sneak out of there without being seen. Suddenly, however, something odd and strange happened, and Daniel forgot about his hunger, as well as about his escape.

Ivanko finished with a loud gulp the contents of Karolek's bottle and threw it away at a nearby tree. The cracking glass shards flew in all directions. Blood appeared on the shepherd's face, and the smiling Karolek simply said:

"Bad."

Ivanko got up with a lot of effort. While leaning on his walking stick, he drew with staggering steps near the fool who was just getting ready to start the next round of the game. Ivanko grabbed the cards from him and threw them up in a wide arch. The cards flew around and then drifted down like heavy leaves.

He then started to swing his cane around wildly, yelled unintelligible words, and staggered and swayed from leg to leg until he fell with all of his weight down on the ground while making a rumbling sound. He tried to get up but fell again on his back. Suddenly, his entire body shook as he started to cry.

Initially, it was only possible to hear an undecipherable roar that sounded like the voice of a wounded animal. But then a desperate wailing came out of his rattling throat:

"Margita!"

On his drunken face, wounded from the shard from the broken bottle, a narrow stream of blood was flowing from his temple down to his mouth through which the moaning words were making their way.

"Why did you leave me, Margita? Why did you do that?"

Karolek placed his giant paws on Ivanko's shoulders, which

were still shaking as he wept. But Ivanko pushed him harshly away, sat halfway up, and loudly yelled:

"I will kill! I will kill him!"

The giant was calming him down, was wiping the blood off his face, and was swinging his oval head that was smiling as always: "Good, good."

But the ominously prominent curved vein on the shepherd's forehead did not hide among the weather-beaten wrinkles.

"I will kill!" he yelled. "Do you hear me? I will kill him! He stole. He stole her from me. The dog! That comedian! He stole my Margita! My beautiful, white Margita. I will kill him!"

He started to cough, turned his face to the ground, and banged his forehead on the turf while weeping.

Daniel held his breath so that he would not miss a word. He trembled with anticipation from being so close to the mystery, the mystery which he was trying so hard to puzzle together from the curses, wails, and shouts that were falling like heavy boulders from the shepherd Ivanko's mouth. There was some woman here. It was Ivanko's wife. Margita. Beautiful, white Margita. And there was also a man here, a man evil like a dog, some comedian who stole Margita from Ivanko.

Stone by little stone, Daniel put together an awful mosaic in his mind. But he did not get too far.

Ivanko was tossing the sentences of his confession onto the muggy and parched land as if throwing stones high to the sky.

"I will kill!" he yelled. "I will kill you, you devil!"

He touched the little red stream near his mouth, and once he saw the blood on his palm, he slowly got up, lifted his reddish hand high, and moaned: "Here! Take it! Take my blood, you devil, and give me back my Margita!"

He reeled again, fell down rumbling as if struck by thunder, and wept a lot of bitter tears.

Daniel trembled. On his glowing cheeks, he felt the heat of tears. In his tight throat, he could taste the salt.

Suddenly, Ivanko got up angrily and, while holding his cane, ran towards Karolek, who was just squatting and was aimlessly swinging his oval and bald head painted with his expressionless smile.

"I will kill!" he rattled. "I will kill."

Karolek instinctively covered his eyes and thus caught the shepherd's stick. He then rose up and slowly walked backward and rumbled: "Bad, bad." Suddenly, he turned around and started to run. The barking dog followed him, but once he noticed that his master fell down, he returned. He remained standing above the drunkard's body and licked the blood from his cheek.

Daniel was quietly sobbing. Pronounced pity mixed in his young heart with childish fears. The glimpse through which he encountered the adult world seemed to be really frightening. He was scared. The bloody drunkard's face horrified him. He was getting goosebumps from the shepherd's threats. He was dizzy and felt like vomiting from the bad breath of events coming to him through the fissure between Ivanko's lips. But there was more pity than fear in him.

Pity for yesterday's bogey man who had turned into a poor wretch.

Pity for a fellow who sold himself to hell only to be deceived by the devil.

Pity for a big man who was crying like a child.

Pity for a mountain of a man whose tears would melt the heart of the devil, if he existed.

But it was clear now that there was no devil. Margita was stolen from Ivanko, not by a devil, but by an evil man.

There are no demons. There are only bad and evil people who hurt others and are not punished for it. Even God does not punish them. But why?

Daniel leaned with his forehead on the tree behind which he was hiding and bitterly wailed.

So the boy Daniel and the shepherd Ivanko wept close to each other, and their tears and Ivanko's blood were the only moisture for the parched and dry soil.

The sun was rising – it was almost noon. The shepherd stood up from the ground, and with still staggering steps, went downhill on the pasture and directed the cattle to a shadier place. Gipsy wagged his shaggy tail with joy and barked at the cows, which were slowly getting up from the warmed-up ground.

Daniel watched the herd for a while as they started to move, guided by Ivanko's staggering gait. Then, he wiped his tearful eyes with his hand and bent down to the blueberry shrub. As he gathered the dark berries and walked around the corner of the forest to the road, he felt hungry and broke into a sprint towards home.

Chapter 2

Farmers

At six in the morning, the farmers started to come out with hoes and spades over their shoulders, and with flasks in their hands. Behind them walked the women, some of them with panniers on their back, others carrying metal containers with plant louse spray. They got up towards the vineyards on the road bypassing the church. At its entrance, the women made the sign of the cross.

Their naked calves were shining in the rising sun. The guys were shamelessly and loudly shouting lewd jokes at them. The women smiled in reply, and their laughter mixed in the morning air with the cock crowing.

But the smiles and jokes began to diminish as they passed the last buildings and approached the fields. The view was depressing. On the ground, there was a fist-thick, parched, solid, and stale film from dried-up mud that was suffocating the soil underneath it. Only a few poor and weak ears of grain penetrated through it but were overshadowed by yellow weeds. In large sections, only stones were seen on the surface. The grain was already plowed in some places, but in other places, its ears were droopingly bowed down under the weight of the muggy days, which continued week after week without any change. It rained a little once or twice, but the drops were only just enough to wash the dust from the stalks. No water, however, seeped through the hardened core to the fine soil.

Already for the second summer, the drought was choking the land. Already for the second summer, they could save only potato patches and some beet and corn. Last year, they were at least able to harvest and sell vine grapes. But this year, as if the plague of the drought were not enough, the vineyards were infected by blight. They were daily trying to fight the deadly disease that was endangering the vine roots in the vineyards, the vineyards on which they pinned their last hopes.

While they walked on the road around the fields, they did not talk much. Just once in a while, they exchanged meaningless words, crushed the dried-up grain between fingers, cursed over the parched soil, and quietly continued on their way. However, as they were nearing the vineyards, their unrest was growing. Those hills threatened to change their poverty – which was bad enough on its own – into the horror of hunger. Anger caused by these unjust rewards for years of hard labor and fear of being unable to feed their own children started to coarsen their speech.

The path up the hill was becoming narrower. Only two people could walk next to each other here, so they split into smaller groups. Gabaňa with old Tomík walked in front, followed by limping Gavora. The space between them and the rest was slowly widening.

"So tell me. You went to the Calvary?" Gavora bitterly raised his voice behind Tomík's back.

The skinny beanpole who used to lead the singing during processions did not even glance back. Only Gabaňa looked over his shoulder as if he was trying to tell Gavora to leave the old man alone. But Gavora just waved his hand.

"You sang a nice song, did you? And you got the rain by praying, didn't you?"

"Stop it, Pišta," said Gabaňa, but Tomík was calming him down with his singsong voice:

"Just leave him. Leave him alone."

"Just leave me," mimicked Gavora. "Just leave me alone. God will punish me! Won't he? But why does he also punish you? Well, well, I blaspheme and am an old sinner. But why isn't my field the only dry one? Why is it not raining at least on yours?"

"The Lord God punishes evil, but sends difficult trials to his devout," replied Tomík without glancing back. But Gavora started to laugh:

"It will help you. It will really help you. I will perish because

God is punishing me. But you will die from hunger because he sends difficult trials to you. That is what you meant?" Gavora laughed with his wild and sour smile.

"Do not worry. We will not die from hunger," said Gabaňa.

"No? And what if blight destroys all of our vineyards? What will we do then?"

"Our vineyards will not be destroyed."

"No? And what will prevent it? The Virgin Mary? Or a miracle?"

Gabaňa did not answer, but it was possible to hear Tomík's singsong voice:

"God will help us."

"What? God will help?" shouted an enraged Gavora. "God will help? Shit will help! Do you hear me? Shit will help! You should have prayed less, and manured more. Manure would have done better for our vineyards than Our Father."

"Don't blaspheme," said Gabaňa seriously. And old Tomík made the sign of the cross and looked up to heaven as if he was praying: "Forgive him, oh Lord, for he does not know what he is doing."

A few steps behind them walked old Okáník, with a yellow walrus mustache through which he muttered his lamentations.

"We will die, we will die, like hungry dogs, we will die. The devil will take our vineyards as well as us. We will perish."

His daughter Nasťa, who walked behind him with her husband, tried to soothe him: "Oh Dad, why do you always complain? In one way or another, we'll carry through."

Martin smiled at the wife on his side, and affectionately glanced at her belly, which was getting bigger, and at her skirt, which could not hide the new life anymore.

The others were catching up to them. Behind them, they heard the wild cursing of Jožka Klvaňa, and a reassuring voice of sickly Palo Markovič.

Once they reached the vineyards, each of them separated into their own lots. They fortified themselves with drinks from their flasks and set off to work. The women were spraying bushes with a plant louse poison, and the men were uncovering the vine roots to see how far the blight had progressed.

Gabaňa, with his sleeves rolled up, was taking the affected roots in his hands and was cutting off the infected branches with his knife. He dug up dried-up bushes and carried them to the pile near a low wall where they would be burnt. Bent with his elbows deep in the soil, he separated healthy roots from the sick ones.

Behind the white wall to which he was taking the uprooted bushes, Gabora was hoeing his own vine. He straightened up, stretched his back, and called towards his neighbor:

"Dig up everything! Burn up everything! Manure again and plant again! But before the new vine produces any grapes, we all will die from hunger."

He spat into his palms and took a swing with his hoe at the bush he was trying to uproot.

Old Tomík, working in another lot, took off the hat, wiped the sweat from his forehead, and made the sign of the cross.

Chapter 3

Philip Taub

At seven o'clock, old Ferenčák appeared in the streets. He fulfilled multiple roles, including a mailman, a bailiff, a public announcer, and a night watchman of the town whose fathers were well-known misers. According to some accounts, many years ago, they even built the gallows on the hill behind the town and were hanging their own sons as they could not afford a hangman. But it was a long time ago, only a charred beam was left from the gallows, and Gipsies were camping on the hilltop. But the frugality of fathers was inherited by their sons. Thus, even when poverty was not hanging over the land like an ominous cloud yet, Ferenčák had diverse assignments throughout the day. In the morning, at seven o'clock, he delivered the mail. At ten o'clock, he hung the drum around his shoulders, walked from corner to corner, beat with drumsticks, removed some paper out of the pocket in his coat, and put glasses with metal frames on his serious face. Then he read with his raucous voice various public announcements from the town council to the gathered boys and women with little babies in their arms. Late afternoon he again exchanged the drum for the postal knapsack, and in the evening stood on the corner in front of Kohút's pub. From there, he dragged a drunken Gipsy to the lock-up or tanked-up fathers of the town to the equally unpleasant arms of their spouses. Once he finished his daily routine, he walked around the streets, blew on an old bull's horn, and sang softly: "Twelve o'clock struck, all souls praise the Lord."

As poverty spread through the countryside, Ferenčák was less and less busy in the evenings as people could not afford to buy booze, and the pub keeper Kohút refused to serve on credit. Otherwise, Ferenčák's duties did not change. Only in his postal knapsack was he carrying more collection notices, and while drumming on the corners, he announced more auctions. Otherwise, nothing changed.

That morning, Ferenčák was passing around the yellow one-story house with the store. Above its entrance hung a metal plate with a partly discolored sign:

PHILIP TAUB
GLAZIER AND GROCER

The door next to the store opened, and a small elderly man came out. His figure was somewhat hunched, and he was wearing a shiny coat with drooping shoulders and long sleeves. He had a faded black bowler hat on his head, tilted to the side, and under his arm, he was carrying a velvet pouch with a prayer book and tefillin prayer straps.

"Good morning, Little Philip," Ferenčák greeted him, as Philip Taub was known by that nickname to all his neighbors.

"Good morning. Do you have anything for us?" replied the man with the black hat in a soft and always kind voice, and his brown dachshund ambled on his short legs towards Ferenčák and greeted him by the friendly wagging of his tail.

"I do have something here," said Ferenčák, and then grabbed a letter from his postal knapsack, and handed it to Philip. Philip briefly looked at the envelope, and as he realized that it was only a bill for the glass, he put it in his pocket without opening it and set out down on the way towards Creekside Street.

At its corner stood baker Spitzer who was already waiting for the mailman. But Ferenčák just waved his hand above his head.

"Nothing again," Spitzer shrugged his broad shoulders with disappointment, and his slow swaying strides joined the short and shuffling but faster steps of Philip.

"Why is the boy not writing?" Spitzer shook his friendly oval head covered with a green straw hat.

"Why is the boy not writing?" he repeated. He could not

believe it.

"Perhaps it will arrive tomorrow," Philip soothed him.

And the same story was repeated every day. Once they passed Creekside Street and reached the town square, Philip knocked on the window of the second house from the corner where Gabriel Menasse lived. An angular face surrounded on three sides by the white beard of a patriarch and on the fourth side by the bright brim of a black hat appeared in the window.

Soon after that, a bulky man with a strict face amplified by his thick ginger eyebrows came out of the house.

"Yitzhak has not written yet," announced sad Spitzer to Gabriel.

"What ingratitude. That is how children are paying back for your kindness," said Gabriel, his resounding prophetic voice ringing in the narrow side street through which they passed from the town square on their way to the synagogue.

"It will for sure arrive tomorrow," Philip tried to calm Spitzer down while looking reproachfully at Gabriel and while making gestures behind the baker's back, trying to convince him to stay silent.

And the same story was repeated every day.

Philip and Gabriel were close friends since their childhood. They learned how to read and write together, and the late Rebbe Mendel, God bless his memory, revealed to both of them the secrets of the sacred books. Since that time, there was probably not a single day that those two odd friends would not meet. Odd as it would be difficult to imagine two persons who resembled each other less than Philip Taub and Gabriel Menasse. Gabriel was an upright giant with a forked figure resembling a spreading tree, whereas Philip was a small, hunched man who looked to the ground. But Philip's humble goodness was clearly becoming more apparent in contrast with Gabriel's stern directness, which did not lose its rigid strength over the passing years.

The strange pair looked like a massive oak and a tiny bent willow, growing next to each other, whose roots were connected somewhere under the surface and were fed by the same sap. In fact, they also argued, and they argued often. But in truth, only Gabriel argued while Philip showed his disagreement by staying quiet or shrugging his sorrowful shoulders or with a pitiful glance at his friend's error. Those glances steamed Gabriel up even further. But no bad word was ever uttered among them, and Philip was the only man in front of whom Gabriel was willing to take off his patriarchal mask and whom he asked for advice.

Gabriel owned a small malting house. His late father, Jacob Menasse, God bless his memory, after whom Gabriel's oldest son was named, was a poor tailor with twelve children. Defiant and proud young Gabriel forced himself to work hard to get a better life than that of his father. By the age of thirty-five, his hard labor and discipline paid off and led to substantial savings, which allowed him to purchase a malting house from old Max Neuer, who moved to Vienna to spend his retirement with his son. In a few years, he transformed an unprofitable and neglected business into a thriving enterprise that provided his family with financial security without any significant worries. That satisfied Gabriel's ambitions, and he had no desires for further expansion or enlargement of his business. He made agreements with several minor farmers for getting every year all the barley he needed. He took care of a brewer responsible for proper malt germination and kilning and then sold the malt to two nearby breweries. Once that was arranged, he did not care for anything else. He spent his time sitting in an old armchair from the black and already worn-off leather, smoked one of his many pipes, which he hung in three rows on the shelf above the armchair and read sacred books. So he sat and puffed and read from the time he got back home from shul in the morning till sunset. His wife Theresa, a tiny, quiet, and somewhat timid lady, tiptoed around him and would only put her small, worn-out hand on his shoulder if some guidance from him was needed.

"Gabriel, Gabaňa is here. He wants advance for the barley."

And Gabriel would look up from his book, would take the pipe out of his mouth, and would either say "Pay him!" or "Send him away!". And Theresa would leave the room to fulfill Gabriel's order, and Gabriel would get back to reading sacred books.

Theresa gave Gabriel four sons: Jacob, Moshe, Ruben, and David. Jacob married Rebecca, the daughter of the tinsmith Kahan, against Gabriel's wishes, as Kahan's son Sigmund was weak in his head. He often walked around the town and asked whomever he encountered why we called a stove a stove or a house a house. But Gabriel gave in to the pleas from his firstborn son, and Rebecca thus became Jacob's wife.

Moshe married the merchant Samuel Klein's daughter, but he continued to live in his father's home, like Jacob. They both worked at the malting house.

Only Ruben married into the home of Abeš Tolnai, a basket and brush maker, and learned the trade from him. The youngest son, David, wedded Chana, the only daughter of Philip Taub, and she gave him his son Daniel.

The sons of Gabriel Menasse were strong and well built like their father, and when the war started, the Emperor of Austria drafted all of them for his armies. Only three came back. The youngest, David, disappeared without a trace. They were told that he was captured by Russians, but the fighting had ended a long time ago, months passed by, and the prisoners of the war returned home, but David was not among them. At that time, Philip Taub's wife, Malka, also died suddenly, and lonely Chana, together with her boy Daniel, returned to her lonely father.

Philip Taub inherited from his father a small store where you could buy candies and a spinning top as well as an oil lamp or a headscarf and a dimity for an eiderdown.

Philip's father was a holy man who did not pay too much attention to his business. He spent all his days with his sacred books and walked to the surrounding Jewish communities to perform a solemn ritual of circumcision. He was known far and wide for his skills as a mohel. He was also known to leave the money he received from the rich for performing a ritual in the cradles at the houses of the poor. But his wife Caroline was a practical woman who took care of the store as well as the household, and advised her sons to learn some trade. Philip completed his apprenticeship as a glazier while Simon became a furrier and moved to Vienna, but died there soon after the passing of his mother.

Philip thus lived alone with his daughter and his grandson Daniel. Chana kept a watch on the household and the store. Philip walked around the town with the pannier on his back while glazing the windows or stood at the large table in the room behind the store, measured and cut the glass, kneaded clods of the putty that smelled nicely like varnish and glazed the frames of the mirrors and the pictures of saints brought to him by the local farmers. He devoted only a short time to reading the sacred books during his day, but he could meditate about what he read while working. He had to work all the time and was unable to just sit still. If there was nothing to do, he always found some meaningful activities. He would sort the goods on the shelves in the store, make necessary repairs to the hen-house in the backyard, pour some milk into the bowl for the cats, bring soup to the poor widow Grün who lived just two streets from their house, or seat Daniel on the large table in his workshop and play Tick-Tack-Toe with him, using black and white beans, or a new game he invented which they called eke-meke-streke.

Towards the evening, they would carry the chairs out to the front of the house. Philip and his daughter would then sit down and cheerfully watch their boy Daniel as he played with the dog Dak on the street. Somewhat later, Gabriel and Theresa would join them, and Daniel would bring more chairs to the front of the house. They sat and talked about the golden times that had passed, as well as the bad times they currently lived through. They talked about everything. Theresa would even timidly drop some gossip, and once they shared all their thoughts, they would quiet down and look at the stars in the sky. Sometimes Philip would take a stroll, and he was sometimes able to convince

Gabriel to join him. Gabriel would then get up from his sacred books and walk with his hands behind his broad back next to Philip's short but fast steps. They would go through Creekside Street up towards the Small Grove and talk about God, His goodness and strictness, about His justice and mercy. Once per week, on Sunday afternoons, they met either in the Philip's or Gabriel's house and with the baker Spitzer, they played a kreuzer mariáš together.

The last out of the three old men who walked so early in the day towards the synagogue for morning prayers was a widower who raised two sons by himself. Older Nathan, who used to help his father in the bakery, was killed during the war. The younger Yitzhak, whose mother Rosa died when he was born, moved to America years ago and wrote two to three times per year. His letters indicated that he was pretty content and prosperous. Yitzhak continued with the trade he had learned from the father, and once he saved enough money, he established a bakery in Brooklyn, got married, and already had two children. A year ago, he sent their photo to the old father for his birthday. Philip framed the picture, and it hung above Spitzer's bed now. For the last time, he wrote at Rosh Hashanah. He read in the newspaper about difficult times in his former homeland and decided to come to visit his father whenever he would be able to leave. Does his father need anything? Could he help him in any way? Old Spitzer answered at that time that he had everything he needed and that he was happy to hear that Yitzhak and his loved ones were doing well. He only asked Yitzhak to write more often.

Many months, however, passed since that time, and Yitzhak did not reply. Every morning, Ferenčák just waved the hand above his head and thus indicated that no letter arrived. That made old Spitzer always quite sad, and he just repeated in disbelief: "Why is the boy not writing?" Philip soothed him every day: "Perhaps it will arrive tomorrow." But Gabriel commented: "What ingratitude. That is how children are paying back for your kindness." And Philip was always making gestures behind sad

Spitzer's back, trying to convince Gabriel to stay silent.

And the same story was repeated every day.

At the end of the narrow road, the old men turned right into the oval opening in the white wall that surrounded the synagogue's courtyard. They entered in quiet solemnity.

The dog followed his master from a respectful distance, he slowly ambled behind the old men, then he stopped, had a sniff of the trunk of the only tree in the street in front of the synagogue's entrance, made his morning ritual, and then laid down in the shade of the stone wall.

Chapter 4

Morning Prayer

It was already quite busy in the courtyard in front of the synagogue. On the bench next to the wall sat a skinny Lebenhart, a retired teacher, and a tinsmith Kahan and between them a butcher Beinhacker, a sturdy fifty-year-old with a bull neck and reddish-blue veined cheeks. His hairy hand played with the massive watch chain on the vest, which remained unbuttoned above his large belly.

Others stood around in small groups. It was possible to see Rabbi Kupfer, a tall man with a full black beard that gave his face a special dignity, sickly and soft-spoken cantor Hercka, shammash Rév with his rusty-red beard and freckled cheeks who had six children (the oldest was just eight years old), wagoner Fischer, a beanpole with an awkward gate, old and toothless brush-maker Abeš Tolnai, his son-in-law, Gabriel's son Ruben Menasse, textile merchant Samuel Klein, Sigmund, a feeble-minded son of tinsmith Kahan, and the skinny and always worried tailor Šefránek.

Beinhacker removed a turnip watch from the pocket in his vest and said as if in passing but loud enough so that everybody could hear him:

"Well, then. Where is our dear Rosh Hakol?"

"This is unheard of to let all of us wait so long," remarked the retired teacher Lebenhart, raising his voice. His gall bladder was bothering him. He did not feel well and was quite bitter, even if there was no reason for being angry.

"This is unheard of," he repeated. "He is supposed to be the first one here, but he comes as the last. It is then not surprising that the kehilla is in such a poor shape," he added with outrage.

Gabriel Menasse moved his bulky figure a few steps closer and stopped in front of the bench where old Lebenhart sat, next to the butcher and the tinsmith. Everybody fell silent once they heard Gabriel's resonant voice.

"Who gave you the right to be angry?" he turned to Lebenhart, whose face became yellowish. "Why are you so mad? What are you doing for the kehilla so that it would look differently? And where is your dear son? And where is your dear son-in-law? Does the shul mean anything to them? And you yourself, if you did not eat so much *treif,* your stomach would not hurt, and you would be less upset."

"This is unheard of, this is unheard of, me and treif," suffocated Lebenhart with anger.

"Treif or no treif, the Rosh Hakol should be here," Kahan said, standing up for Lebenhart.

"That's right," Beinhacker seconded him. "Is he here? No. He is not. And who is responsible for the fact that our kehilla is falling apart? Well, then. Who?"

"We all are responsible," thundered Gabriel, and the eyebrows on his ruddy face got even thicker.

The disgruntled grumbling resonating through the courtyard was suddenly interrupted by the voice of the teacher, who had pulled himself back together by then:

"And why do you dare to ask me about my son? Where are your Jacob and Moshe? Where?" Lebenhart looked triumphantly around.

"That's none of your business. They had to drive to the brewery in the morning. But they took their tefillin with them." Gabriel's voice did not sound too convincing as he knew that he was not telling the whole truth. He really sent Moshe in the morning with the barley, but Jacob stayed at home. When Gabriel thought about the indignity he suffered as he was forced to lie, his forehead wrinkled. But he turned his anger against Beinhacker.

"I am telling you – Timfeld is the best man we have. He does all he can. And you will never become a Rosh Hakol even if you walked on your head."

The butcher jumped up and ran towards Gabriel.

"Rosh Hakol? Who wants to be a Rosh Hakol?" he yelled, and the veins on his bull neck were becoming more prominent.

"You want to be a Rosh Hakol," answered Gabriel, and his voice became firm again.

"Me and a Rosh Hakol? Not even if you begged me!"

"My friends, don't argue here. Not at this place," Philip tried to calm down the raging parties.

But at that moment, Aaron Timfeld, a sawmill owner and a farmer, and a chairman of their congregation, called Rosh Hakol, walked into the courtyard. He was a broad-backed middle-aged man with calm, intelligent, and level-headed eyes on his shaven and weather-beaten face. Behind him minced a traveling salesman Ignatius Kantůrek who was making, with his squeaky voice, a thousand excuses for coming late and even delaying their Rosh Hakol.

"Let's pray," said Aaron Timfeld as he entered the synagogue. Shammash Rév was already inside, where he was taking care of the chest hiding the rolls of the sacred Scripture behind a red velvet curtain with the Star of David embroidered in gold.

They sat down in the pews, each at his own place. Beinhacker glanced once more angrily at Gabriel before the whining and shaky tenor of Cantor Hercka started the prayers.

Whenever the cantor stumbled while reading the Torah, the butcher corrected him in a loud voice from his place in the first pew, clicked his tongue twice, and shook his head from side to side to show how surprised he was that the cantor could make those mistakes. But that was nothing unusual, and nobody in the synagogue paid attention. Only wagoner Fischer sometimes answered Beinhacker's smack with even louder, sharper, and exhortative "Psst!" The butcher then turned and said to his neighbor Lebenhart loudly enough so that others could hear it: "Nebbish."

The same story was repeated every day except on the Sabbath, and high holidays as even Beinhacker valued their solemnity more than his enmity towards Timfeld. On the Sabbath, Hercka could make as many mistakes as he wished. But every other day, he had to be careful. And as it was not the Sabbath today, it was not unusual for the butcher Beinhacker to loudly correct all the cantor's stumbles.

But something extraordinary still happened today after Rabbi Kupfer concluded the services and blessed the congregation while holding in his raised arms the fringes of the black and white tallit. The lingering sound of "*Yevarechecha*" was still in the air as people started to leave their pews when Beinhacker approached the chairman of the congregation, Timfeld, and shouted so that everybody could hear him:

"Well, then. And when will our dear Rosh Hakol tell us how much money is left in kehilla's treasury?"

Timfeld just looked at him with his blazing intelligent eyes and said: "Our situation is bad."

He then turned around towards the exit door. But the butcher grabbed his sleeve and tried to harass him further:

"Bad? That's all you are willing to share? Bad! Bad! We all know that the kehilla is falling apart. If it continues like that, our kehilla will come under the hammer. But our dear Rosh Hakol just says 'bad' and walks away as if everything were great."

"That is unheard of," seconded Lebenhart, who sprang back to life as he found a new opportunity for arguing.

Aaron Timfeld pushed down Beinhacker's hand as they stood against each other like two angry bulls who were sizing each other up. The butcher's eyes became bloodshot, and his purple-veined cheeks turned red. They would almost have started to fight, but the small figure of Philip Taub placed himself between them and separated them. He then approached Beinhacker and reminded him in a strong and surprisingly firm voice:

"Do not forget that you are in the house of God."

The unusual and surprising strictness of Philip's voice forced Beinhacker to turn around. Like a beaten and dejected animal, he was discontentedly grumbling as he was getting ready to leave the kehilla's holy home. But Philip stopped him again and said:

"Do not worry. Our kehilla will not come under the hammer. We will not allow that. You will be the first one who will not allow it."

It was again that old, soft and shaky, but soothingly pleasant voice of Philip Taub for which he was known. Aaron Timfeld's eyes regained their peace.

"Beinhacker is right," he said, and he never gained as much respect in his congregation as after that admission. "Beinhacker is right. I should have told you a long time ago. But I did not want to make you worried. I know that each one of you has a lot to worry about. The kehilla is almost bankrupt. Our treasury is empty. Next month I will pay for everything with my own money. But my fields are not more fruitful than yours. I cannot afford to do that for too long. Beinhacker is right. We must get together. And we have to find some solution." And as if he suddenly decided, he added: "Let's meet tomorrow after mincha."

Everybody agreed, and they started to leave for their homes. When Philip exited with Gabriel and the baker Spitzer through the oval entrance in the stone wall that separated the synagogue courtyard from the street, Dak slowly got up from the shade and swayed on his short legs behind his master.

Chapter 5

Gabriel Menasse

When the boy Daniel got back home from his expedition to uncover Ivanko's secrets, Kate was already serving the soup. It was a bean soup which Daniel did not like, but today he ate it all, down to the very last spoonful without saying a word. He did not react when Mother complained that he was late. And when Grandpa Philip tried to ask with a smile on his face where he was wandering around the entire morning, he just gave an evasive answer.

He was glad when Mother asked him after the lunch to bring Grandma Theresa a borrowed poppy-seed grinder. He always liked visiting Grandpa Gabriel, whose collection of painted pipes he could admire, and his Grandma Theresa who gave him sweets. But this time he was also glad to go there for other reasons. He was glad because he wanted to be alone. He was still processing in his tousled head what he saw and heard today in the morning up on the pastures at the Wet Grove. He wanted to sort it out in his mind. He wanted to be alone.

In front of the house at the edge of the sidewalk, Jura Tomík sat and played with little stones. He gathered four pebbles in front of him on the sidewalk, threw one of them up, and quickly grabbed the remaining three, and then caught the fourth one while it was still in the air. Then, he threw two and promptly captured the remaining two before catching the falling stones. When he saw Daniel, he asked him to go with him to the river to catch the tadpoles. But today, Daniel was not in a mood for such silliness!

He started on the way but did not pick up the shortest route. He did not go through Creekside Street but turned left instead and ran through the avenue of the lime trees leading up to the chapels on the Calvary Hill. While there, he sprawled on the grass at the hillside. He picked up a blade and chewed on it, looked up at the blue sky, and tried to think everything through.

One thing was clear. There is no devil. Grandfather Philip was right. Bogeymen and demons are only in fairy tales. The man who stole Margita from Ivanko was not a devil but just an evil man. But why does God allow evil people to hurt the good ones? Cantor Hercka says that God is almighty. He could thus prevent evil people from hurting the good ones. Grandfather Gabriel says that God is just. But in that case, why does he not punish the evil man who stole Margita from Ivanko? And Grandfather Philip says that God is merciful. Why does he show no mercy to Ivanko? Why does he only look from heaven at Ivanko's weeping, and why doesn't he help him?

Daniel picked up another blade of grass, spat out the chewed one, turned on his belly, and with his back towards heaven, continued to lead a conversation with the incomprehensible God. It was not only about Ivanko. Daniel knew that there were many unfortunate people in the world. What about the widow Grün or the feeble-minded tinsmith's son who was laughed at by children when he walked from house to house asking odd questions? And what about their maid Kate who was limping and whom he once caught crying and who admitted to him that she wept because she would not marry and would have no children because she was crippled? And what about the old Okáník who wailed that a blight destroyed his entire vineyard? And shammash Rév, who did not know how to feed his six children? Why? Why does God only look at their suffering? Why, if he is merciful, does he not pity them, and does he not help them in their misfortune?

God is good, says Grandfather Philip. But why did he send such a bad drought to the land? Why did he cause them to all be poor and hungry? And why, my God, did my father not come back from the war? And why did You allow the war in the first place? Why did You let men kill each other so that women would weep for them like my mom whenever she thinks about Dad? Why?

Daniel was hitting the grass with his fist as if he wanted to force the hill to answer his questions. He almost wanted to weep again as he did in the morning on Ivanko's pasture. But the hill remained silent and refused to give up its secrets. Only a cricket was heard somewhere in the grass as if he was trying to saw a hard and rigid wood. The same sound all the time. He is perhaps also always asking the same question, came suddenly to Daniel's mind. Perhaps all the crickets were always asking the same question. At least they all always sounded the same. One sang higher, others sang lower, but the song was always equally monotonous. Perhaps it was necessary to always ask the same questions. But he was not as patient as the crickets in the grass now. If the slope does not want to share its secret, let it keep it. But he will learn about everything anyway otherwise. Once he grows a little older.

He picked up from the ground the poppy-seed grinder that he was supposed to bring to Grandmother Theresa. He then stuck out his tongue at the silent slope and went downhill. At the foot of the hill, he broke into a run directly to Grandfather Gabriel's house.

It was an old one-story house with flaking stucco and a gateway that was wide enough that a loaded wagon could pass through to the ruggedly paved courtyard fronting the barley storage house. Daniel enjoyed his time inside of that storage house. The scales with weights were there, and he could use those for pretending to be a strongman. The cats Mina and Fina lived there, and he could try to grab their tails. And there were many sacks there, and he could count them. It was comforting to plunge his hand into the warm grain and let it fall from his palm back to the sack.

Whenever Daniel visited Grandfather Gabriel's house, he always stopped in that storage room first. But this time, he just ran up over the three steps leading from the courtyard to the kitchen, handed the poppy-seed grinder over to old Barbara, who served in Grandfather's house as long as Daniel could remember. He entered the big room where his grandfather was sitting, spread out on his armchair. But he was not reading. He picked up one of the well-seasoned porcelain pipes from the shelf and veiled himself in a cloud of smoke.

The table was not yet cleared up after lunch. Grandmother Theresa, Uncle Jacob with his wife, Aunt Rebecca, Uncle Moshe with Aunt Hedwig, and their son, Cousin David, were all still sitting at the table. Theresa's small hands were quickly sewing up a hole in the stocking. Aunt Hedwig was lecturing Cousin David as he sat with his elbows on the table. In the palms of his hands he held up his face, wearing those thick glasses fronting his near-sighted eyes.

"Sit straight! Don't sit like that," Aunt Hedwig told her son.

"Leave him alone," ordered Uncle Moshe, and Aunt Hedwig stared at him with blazing eyes.

Uncle Jacob was sharpening his pencil while Aunt Rebecca sat quietly and stared into space. She kept her hands on her womb, which was giving away the secret that Daniel would soon get another cousin. But her lips were puffy, and to Daniel, she seemed to be uglier than usual.

Daniel greeted them and stopped in front of Grandmother:

"I brought back the poppy-seed grinder. Mother sends her thanks. I left it in the kitchen with Barbara."

"You are a nice boy."

Theresa looked up from her sewing, and her old, wrinkled face with lively eyes and white straight hair parted in the middle, smiled at the boy. Then she got up from the table.

"Wait a moment. I will peel an apple for you."

All of the people, including Theresa, spoke in soft voices. Daniel looked at Grandfather's bristling eyebrows, and he knew right away that Grandpa was having one of his bad days. On other days, whenever Daniel came in, Gabriel looked up from his book, and even if he had seemed to be very serious till that moment, he would have smiled at Daniel, would have touched his hair, and would have asked him: "So what kind of prank have you pulled today?" Daniel was known in the family as the only person able to make Gabriel laugh, and it was attributed to his resemblance with his poor father David, who used to be Gabriel's favorite child.

Today, however, Gabriel did not even look at Daniel. He sat in his armchair and puffed, and later took the pipe out of his mouth only to bite the end of his beard, which was yellowish from the smoke. Nobody guessed the reason for his reticence, and nobody tried to discover it. They knew that the old man would not share the truth with them anyway and that their questioning would just steam him up even further. They thus spoke in soft voices, and Theresa walked on her tiptoes. Whoever was not in shul that morning could not even guess what bothered Gabriel's mind. Moshe would not understand even if he were there that morning with Gabriel as he was not very sharp. If nature had given him the bright intellect of his brothers Jacob or David, he would have guessed what was preying on Gabriel's mind.

It was hurting him as painfully as a hook in the throat of a caught fish since that morning, since the moment he left shul and walked back home after he said goodbye to Philip. And the hook had two sharp tips.

He still saw in front of him the raging faces of Aaron Timfeld and butcher Beinhacker and the tiny figure of Philip Taub, who had placed himself between them and separated them. He still heard in his ears Philip's voice as he turned towards Beinhacker: "Do not forget that you are in the house of God." Only a few words. Without any anger or threats, just those few words from the mouth of a tiny, weak man, who could be instantly thrown by Beinhacker to the ground. And how helpful were those words! And how dejected was Beinhacker when he crawled away. And how ashamed everybody felt. But Philip immediately found the words that put everybody's shame to rest. If Gabriel were in charge, he would have punished Beinhacker with his own hands. He would have jumped at his throat, would have strangled him, and would have beaten the evil out of his soul. But Philip? While Gabriel was clenching his fists, Philip just said a few words. And Gabriel knew that those words were better and more effective than his fists would have been had he gathered the courage to use them.

Philip and Gabriel were bound by an old friendship. But also by an old fight. They argued so many times whether God was merciful or just, whether he forgave the sinners or punished those who broke his laws, an eye for an eye, a tooth for a tooth, till the third or fourth generation. How many times he got angry at his old friend when he tried to convince him that people were not evil, just imperfect. How many times he laughed at Philip when he claimed that a kind word told with humility was a more powerful weapon than a fist or a whip. And how many times did Philip convince him about that as clearly as this morning? But something inside him always prevented him from accepting that truth. His world would fall apart if the Lord God did not punish the sin and injustice with a flaming sword. If the godless and evildoers were allowed to rely on God's mercy and forgiveness. If those who walked in fear of God had no right to punish in the name of God the sinners, the godless, and the arrogant. But what would he have achieved if he had thrown the butcher to the ground? Would he have just poured more oil into the fire? Were not Philip's few words better? But why did Philip never rush things, why did he always know what to do, why did he never lose his composure, in contrast to Gabriel, who was always overwhelmed by his first emotion? Today in the morning, Philip not only won over the butcher. He also won over him, and awareness of that defeat known only to Gabriel filled him with unrest.

But the second tip of the double hook was hurting Gabriel's wounded heart even more. Today in the morning, he had lied.

Today in the morning, he had to lie. His own son forced him to lie. When teacher Lebenhart asked him maliciously where his sons were and whether the shul was not good enough for them, he gave him an untruthful answer. He knew that early in the morning, only Moshe went with the barley. But he lied that Jacob went with him. He lied. He lied inside the shul. And his own son forced him to lie. True, Philip's merciful God would forgive him. But not the Lord God, the God of Gabriel, whose wrath was everlasting.

While Gabriel mulled over those things veiled in the clouds of fume and biting the end of his beard that was yellowish from the smoke, the boys Daniel and David sat with their legs crossed in the opposite corner of the big room and played Tick-Tack-Toe. Daniel always carried with him an old handkerchief on which he had drawn straight lines needed for the game as well as black and white beans, which they used for the game. David thought everything through and held the bean for a long time in his hand before deciding where to place it. Daniel made decisions fast and got upset at himself whenever he made a mistake, but was usually able to correct any error during his next turn.

The tall clock standing in the corner next to the window showed half-past two. It then stroke one high and three deep strikes. Moshe and Hedwig got up and exited the room. After a while, Theresa put her sewing away and left the lounge too. She went to the kitchen to help Barbara with the dishes. Rebecca collected the remaining plates from the table and followed her mother-in-law. Once Theresa got back, she shook the tablecloth out through the window to remove all the crumbs before carefully folding it up. At that moment, Jacob also got up and was getting ready to leave and join his brother.

Gabriel, however, removed the pipe from his mouth and said:

"I need to talk to you."

Theresa turned around and wanted to go back from the door while still holding the tablecloth. Her eyes indicated how worried she was. She knew how short-tempered Gabriel was and even though she did not know what he wanted to discuss with Jacob, her heart felt an upcoming storm.

"I need to talk to Jacob," said Gabriel impatiently, and Theresa quickly walked out of the room and quietly closed the door behind her.

Once they were alone, Gabriel got up from his armchair and started to walk around the room while still smoking his pipe. Then he suddenly stopped in front of his son, tried to keep his composure, and asked Jacob calmly:

"Why didn't you come to shul this morning?"

Jacob, who was leaning on the table with his hands, looked to the ground and did not answer.

"I am asking you why you didn't go to pray this morning?" repeated Gabriel, his voice getting louder.

Slowly, as if he was trying to turn a boulder which could tumble down with any careless move, Jacob replied:

"I had work to do, Father."

"You had work?" Gabriel repeated after him and was hardly able to control himself. "You had work! Prayer is more important than work. And you know it well. Do not make excuses, tell me the truth. Why didn't you come to shul this morning?"

After a while, Jacob interrupted the tense silence.

"Why do you scold me like a small child?" he asked calmly and in a firm voice. "You for sure know that those things do not mean as much for me as they do for you, Father."

His voice sounded conciliatory, and in the word "Father," one could even hear his timid and hidden love. But Gabriel exploded:

"Does not mean much? And what does it mean for you? Nothing. Nothing. Nothing at all. Service to the Lord God means nothing for my son. For the son of Gabriel Menasse! And you ask me why I scold you? Do I scold you? No. I am just warning you, a godless man, as God punishes those who do not fear him!"

His words fell on Jacob's head like heavy clods of earth. Jacob, however, did not try to avoid the angry look of his father's eyes, and after a while, he continued in a firm voice:

"If I am bad, God will punish me. It is not your task to punish me."

Gabriel again exploded. His entire body was shaking as his fist started to pound on the table.

"You may call God's wrath upon your head. Yes, let God punish you for your godlessness! But hear me, I will punish you as your godlessness inflicts God's wrath on all of us!"

Gabriel yelled. And he raised the hand holding his pipe and pounded it on the edge of the table. The pipe broke. Jacob lost his patience, gritted his teeth, turned around, and ran out of the room.

The old man felt dizzy and grabbed the nearest chair. He then made two faltering steps, and once he reached his armchair, he slowly sat down.

He remained seated with the palm of his hand covering his eyes while breathing heavily. After a while, he stood up, took another pipe from the shelf, filled it, lit it, and then sat down again. He picked up the book on the stool next to the armchair, opened it, and continued to read from where he had ended up. But he read only briefly. He could not focus. And he did not enjoy his pipe either. He put the book aside, knocked out the unfinished pipe, slowly got up, and started to pace around the room with his hands behind his back. Then he replaced his black velvet yarmulke, which was for at-home use, with a hat and left the house. He walked towards Philip Taub's store, and his figure did not seem as straight as usual.

During all that time, the boys Daniel and David sat with their legs crossed in the opposite corner of the big room and played Tick-Tack-Toe. In fact, they had just pretended that they were playing and that they were not paying any attention to what was happening in the world of adults around them. Since Grandfather Gabriel was left alone in the room with Uncle Jacob, both boys listened intently and tried not to miss a single word. They did not focus on their game as they could not think about where to place the third bean in a row or which bean to take away from the opponent. They only thought about Grandfather Gabriel's anger and about what Uncle Jacob would say in reply. When Gabriel started to yell at Jacob, David got really scared and wanted to get up and run away. But Daniel grabbed his shoulder and forced him to stay without saying a word. But as soon as Gabriel loudly shut the door behind him, Daniel quickly looked up from his game, made a wrong move on purpose, and when David took advantage of his mistake, he said:

"So you have won. But I already have to go."

He gathered the beans and the old handkerchief from the floor, got up quickly, and ran out of the room. But he did not go home right away. He passed the courtyard, turned around to make sure that David was not following him, and entered the storage house. While there, he sat down in the dark corner hidden behind the sacks of barley and rested his elbows on his knees while his palms supported his chin.

And he thought again about everything. Grandfather's talk with Uncle Jacob was for the boy like a new thread allowing him to spin, like a new stone to be used to complete a picture he was putting together in his mind. Daniel felt that Uncle Jacob was right. He did not seem to be evil to him. He allowed him to sit on the coachbox outside on the road. He even allowed him to use the reins and the whip. No, Uncle Jacob was not a bad man. He never beat the horses, and talked to them like to the people. And he taught Daniel how to catch fish with cherries. And he recognized all the birds by their sounds. No, Uncle Jacob was not a bad man. And if he was godless, why should Grandfather punish him for it? Let God Himself punish him if He really does not forgive when Uncle Jacob sometimes misses the prayers. Uncle Jacob was right, thought Daniel. Yes, but the worst came later.

Grandfather Gabriel said that because of Uncle Jacob's godlessness, the wrath of the Lord God would fall on all of us. But Grandfather Philip said that God was good. And it would be indeed not good if, for example, baker Spitzer or shepherd Ivanko were punished for Uncle Jacob's godlessness. And it would not be just. And Grandfather Gabriel himself says that God is just. How should he believe that God is just when He punishes everybody, even the innocent, for one sinner? No, it cannot be like that. No, Grandfather was, for sure, not right.

The thread held by Daniel started to fray. Even this stone could not help to complete the picture.

At that moment, the rusty cat Fina that had until now slept somewhere between the sacks, approached Daniel and started to rub her head on his knee. But Daniel angrily pulled her tail. Fina bitterly mewed and ran away as she took offense.

Daniel got up from the ground. He was tired, as if he had worked really hard. But he did not plunge his hand into the warm grain and did not let it shed back from his palm. He just angrily kicked the nearest sack and walked slowly to the open gate leading from the storage house into the courtyard.

Chapter 6

Saving the Synagogue

The next day early in the morning, Theresa, as always, helped Barbara with breakfast and then got out into the courtyard to scatter grain for the hens. As always, she stood up in the center of the courtyard, held a flat basket with the grain next to her hip, scooped it into her tiny cupped hand, and sprinkled the grain on the rugged pavement of the courtyard. She pouted a toothless mouth in a wrinkled face, and her lips made a high-pitched sound: "Chick, chick, chick, chick, chick." The hens immediately gathered around and started to peck.

Once she was finished, however, she did not get back to the three steps leading to the kitchen. She walked through the courtyard to the other end of the house and stopped under the window of the room where Jacob and Rebecca slept. She quietly knocked on the glass with her finger and waited.

After a while, the window opened, and Jacob's unshaven face appeared inside. He was still sleepy, but once he noticed Theresa, his eyes shined.

"What's up, mom?" he asked kindly.

"Jacob," she whispered.

"What's up, mom?" he repeated.

"Jacob, go to pray with father this morning." She spoke in a low voice, her raised eyes imploring him.

Jacob's face became cloudy for a short moment as he recalled yesterday's argument with his father. Then he looked at his mother standing beneath him with an empty flat basket in her hand while raising her eyes towards him with an imploringly worried look on her face. How much he loved her! How could he refuse anything to her? He smiled at her and said:

"You listened behind the door yesterday, didn't you?"

Theresa did not answer. But after a while, she begged again:

"Go with father today, Jacob. Go, my boy. Do it for me."

He smiled at her again and said:

"Do not worry, I will go."

Happy Theresa shook her head veiled with white hair.

"I knew that you were a nice boy. I knew that you would do that for me."

She raised her hand, and her small soft palm timidly touched Jacob as he leaned over the windowsill. Then she quietly left for the kitchen.

That morning when Philip and baker Spitzer reached the house of Gabriel Menasse, and Gabriel came out, Jacob joined them at the gate, and they walked together to the synagogue for the morning prayer service.

Gabriel did not say a word. Jacob was glad that he could so easily appease his mother and that Father did not bring up what happened between them yesterday. Only when baker Spitzer announced in a sad voice that Yitzhak again did not write, and when Gabriel responded as always: "What ingratitude. That is how children pay for your kindness," Jacob felt that this time, the reproach was aimed more at him than at the baker's son. He, however, continued to walk quietly next to the old men and slowed down so that they could keep up with him.

They did not talk much today. Baker Spitzer was becoming more dispirited day by day as old Ferenčák continued to just wave his hand above his head. Jacob did not know what to tell the old men, and was somewhat afraid that his words would upset his father. Philip remained quiet so as not to disturb others in their thoughts, and Gabriel seemed to be absorbed in his own thoughts.

He glanced at Jacob by his side only once in a while, even though his mind was focused on him. What a strange man this firstborn son of his was. How little he understood him. How little he recognized himself in him. People claimed that when he was born, he was a living image of his father. He himself, however, never saw any resemblance. He did not even resemble his brothers. He differed from Moshe. He was brighter, firmer, and faster than him. He differed from Ruben, who was not as dumb as Moshe but was quiet like his mother and was also selfish and followed only his own interests. He differed from poor David, who resembled him due to his shrewdness as well as his prowess but was softer and almost unmanly. No, Jacob did not resemble his brothers. He was always different. It was always more challenging with him. Even as a little boy, he was never satisfied with orders. Whenever he heard "you have to" or "you mustn't," he always had his: "Why, why, why do I have to, why am I not allowed to?" He was not disobedient, but he did not obey to just follow commands. He obeyed because he wanted to obey. Because he wanted to satisfy Theresa's wishes. But once he made up his mind, he did not fear any threats or any punishments. You could beat him as much as you wish, but he did not cry. He was very proud. Yes, in that stubbornness and pride, he probably most resembled his father. How much time he and Theresa spent trying to convince him not to wed Rebecca.

Children usually turned out to be like the mother's brothers, they told him, and her brother was a fool. But even that did not stop him, and he forced his own will through. It was always so difficult with Jacob. He did not spend too much time with books but was very smart. And he was clever with his hands too. Whatever he saw, he was able to replicate. He was also good with people, they liked him and approached him whenever they needed advice.

Gabriel then glanced at Philip, who walked quietly next to him. It seemed to him that Jacob could have been a son of Philip rather than his own. But Philip was devout and feared God, whereas Jacob did not fear anything. Not even God. He never read sacred books. He just wandered over the fields and woods and went fishing from the river's edge, like a goy. Oh well, what a strange man was this firstborn son of his. Even his God, if he had one, is quite different from the God of Gabriel. Even different from the God of Philip. He is not in heaven and does not descend into the sanctuary during the time of prayer, and does not speak through the words of the sacred rolls of the Holy Scripture. He is in the meadows and the woods and the waters and speaks the language of wind and creeks. That is how it is with Jacob, thought Gabriel to himself. It will be something like that. But in that case, why do I force him to praise the Lord with me in shul? Only to soothe the old Lebenhart? Only because of my pride? No, not because of that! I do it as it is written that the Lord God will punish those who do not walk in fear of Him. And his son, son of Gabriel Menasse, cannot, because of his godlessness, bring God's punishment on the entire community. Jacob is indeed stubborn. But I am stubborn, too, and know how to be harsh. I will fight. And should the Lord God order it, I would even sacrifice my son like Abraham.

So they finally reached the synagogue while not uttering a word. During the services, nothing unusual happened... Only Beinhacker from his place in the first pew clicked his tongue loudly several times whenever the cantor stumbled while reading from the Torah, and wagoner once or twice answered the butcher's smack with even a louder, sharper, and exhortative "Psst!" But nobody paid attention to it.

Only once they were leaving the synagogue, Aaron Timfeld reminded them that they would meet today after mincha to discuss how to save the finances of the kehilla.

But nobody needed any reminders. All of them came for mincha, even those who could not join them in the morning. Only Rabbi Kupfer, cantor Hercka, and shammash Rév stepped out after the service, as they knew that the main topic of deliberations would be where the congregation would find the money for their next month's salaries.

Others were loudly getting up from their places and gathered around a long table behind the pews at the back of the synagogue. Aaron Timfeld sat at the head of the table, next to the door on a chair with a high backrest. Once everybody was seated, he twice pounded on the desk with his palm. After they all fell silent, he cleared his throat and began:

"Dear friends, you all know why we have gathered. You know what our situation is. You know that our coffers are empty. We are at the bottom. I promised that next month, I would pay the rabbi, cantor, and shammash on my own. But we are here to decide what to do next. I ask you for your suggestions."

Aaron Timfeld again cleared up his throat and fell silent. He then tugged a handkerchief between his bull neck and collar that seemed to be too small for him. He was not a speaker. He did not like to talk. He liked to act. But he had to first know how to act, and this time he was really not sure. They sat in front of him and waited for his advice. Did they expect miracles from him? There were holes in the roof of the synagogue that had to be repaired. Once the rains start, water will be pouring into the sanctuary. But who will pay the roofer? And who will pay the cantor and shammash and rabbi? And the walls around here would definitely need whitewashing! But who will pay for it?

"Does anybody have any suggestions?" repeated Aaron Timfeld as they all remained quiet, and nobody seemed ready to talk. Timfeld stared hard at the butcher's purple-veined face. That made Beinhacker uneasy, but after a few moments of restless fidgeting, he exploded:

"Suggestions! Suggestions! It is easy to ask for suggestions. Why were we not informed a long time ago that the kehilla was falling apart?"

"Yes, that's right. Why were we not informed before," the teacher sided with Beinhacker.

Timfeld stayed calm this time, and as if he did not hear, he repeated again:

"I am asking if anybody has any suggestions."

After a few additional minutes of awkward silence, Samuel Klein was the first one to speak. He owned a small textile shop at the town square, and when he spoke, he seemed to measure his words as if he measured fabric. After every sentence, he paused as if he was taking another measurement. He proposed to get a mortgage on the synagogue at the local bank. His suggestion was met with enormous backlash.

"No! No! We do not want them to know that we are struggling. Never!" sounded from all sides. Klein shrugged his shoulders, stretched out his hands, and indicated that he was taking the proposal back if others disagreed. But it is not up to him anymore. He made a nice try and is relieved of his responsibilities now.

"Does anybody have any other suggestion?" asked Aaron Timfeld.

Old Lebenhart straightened up in his chair and, once he was sure that everybody's eyes were directed at him, started to talk in a shaky but angry voice:

"Why do we have to have a rabbi, a cantor, and a shammash? Wouldn't just a rabbi and a shammash be enough? Why do we need a cantor? Our rabbi knows how to read from the Torah. Our rabbi knows how to sing. And couldn't he also teach religious classes for our children? Why didn't we fire our cantor a long time ago?" Lebenhart got mad, and his face became yellowish.

"Well then? What does our Rosh Hakol say?" triumphantly pronounced the butcher. "Perhaps our rabbi would not make so many mistakes."

But Aaron Timfeld remained calm and did not lose his temper today.

"What do I say? I say that depriving poor Hercka of bread would not save us. And I also say that nothing like that will happen as long as I am a Rosh Hakol here."

A buzz of approval from all sides of the table put Beinhacker down, but an awkward silence again followed. It was interrupted by the tinsmith Kahan.

"Everything is in vain. We will not invent anything against this misery," he said and helplessly waved his hand.

"Misery is misery," nodded tailor Šefránek in agreement as he had experienced poverty for much longer than others.

The silence again loomed largely, but then the squeaky voice of traveling salesman Kantůrek was heard: "If the gentlemen allow,

I would have an idea. But I ask you upfront, please forgive me a thousand times should you not like it. I meet many people during my travels, and recently, when visiting Břeclav, I encountered an antique dealer Braun who was buying old synagogue articles. I, of course, have not told him anything. I have not uttered a word, but it crossed my mind that should the gentlemen here agree, to put kehilla back on its feet, we could sell some older Torahs and the silver crowns. Perhaps the Mizrach or ..."

Kantůrek did not finish his sentence as a large wave of protests rose in the room and swept the traveling salesman away like a wild wind that sweeps a shell and drowned out his squeaky voice like a sea storm that swallows the chirping of a chicken.

"A sacrilege!" roared Gabriel Menasse, and his fist pounded on the table.

"Impossible!"

"Never!"

"To sell a Torah! That is unheard of!" Lebenhart was losing his temper.

"*Sma 'Jisroel!*" dreaded wagoner Fischer.

The thunderstorm of anger was growing so fast that Aaron Timfeld had to punch the desk to calm everybody down.

"After all, I have not said anything," squeaked Kantůrek apologetically while curled up in his chair in a heap of misery. "Nothing happened, after all, of course. I told you beforehand that we could do that only if the gentlemen here agreed. My intentions were good, of course."

But the flurry caused by Kantůrek's suggestion was too big to even think about continuing with any deliberations. They all got up on their feet, and Aaron Timfeld quickly concluded the meeting with an announcement that they would gather again next week.

"Haven't I said that?" mentioned Kahan at the exit door. "Against this misery, we will not invent anything."

"That's right. Misery is misery," nodded the tailor.

Toothless Abeš Tolnai spread out his hands: "Why did we eat the frogs?" And he started to tell the anecdote about two Jews who walked through the forest and saw a frog. The first one made a bet that he would eat that frog if he got ten crowns as a reward. The second one agreed, and once the first one ate the frog, he gave him ten crowns. They continued to wander through the woods and again encountered a frog. The second one made the same bet now, and the first one accepted the challenge. The second one then ate the frog, and the first one gave him his ten crowns back. And then they asked each other: Why did we eat those frogs after all?

It was an old joke, everybody knew it, but nobody laughed. They were still too upset. To sell the Torah! To sell the Mizrach! They appeared to walk out of a funeral. No – out of a murder scene.

That entire evening, they did not talk about anything else. Even when they brought the chairs on the porch and looked at the starlit skies. Even when they went to bed at night, they did not think about anything else. To sell the Mizrach! To sell the Torah! It continued to occupy their minds. They fell asleep uneasily, like after a blaze.

Only Jacob Menasse considered Kantůrek's suggestion wise. But he kept his thoughts to himself.

Chapter 7

Rebecca

Jacob woke up at sunrise. It was Sunday, and he did not have to get up early. He thus stayed in bed with eyes wide open and looked at the ceiling. The first fly entered the room through the opened window and buzzed above him. It then sat on the pillow next to Rebecca's head, and Jacob waved it away. He then looked at his wife, who was still asleep next to him.

She laid on her back, with only her head leaning against her naked shoulder. Her lips were puffy, and at the end of her swollen eyelids, short and spiky eyelashes loomed up. Her sweaty hair was falling over her forehead, and her tired breath was passing through her half-opened mouth. She shook off the blanket while asleep, and from the décolleté of her nightgown, a tallow-colored breast fell out, and her heavy pregnant body laid motionlessly next to Jacob.

She is not pretty anymore, thought Jacob. Was she ever pretty? He liked her before they got married. Oh God, how much they wanted each other, he said to himself. But where is it now? Where is everything? How did it vanish? On the sky behind the opened window, there was still a pale narrow crescent of the descending moon in its last quarter. Their love was slowly disappearing, like the moon that is narrowing into the darkness, he thought. But with the moon, you know that it will start to grow again tomorrow. But with him and Rebecca, it is different. They have laid next to each other night after night for three years already. And for three years, he wakes up every morning next to her body which he had stopped liking a long time ago. It is true, he had to admit, there were many beautiful nights, but mornings were never different from this one. Perhaps he should have really listened to his father, who had advised him to not marry Rebecca. Perhaps he was right. But at that time, he liked her, and they wanted each other. They wanted each other so much. But who knows? Perhaps it is the same with all the women. Perhaps it would not be different if he had listened and found somebody else.

In the courtyard, under the window, the cock crowed. Jacob jumped from his bed, stretched his arms and legs, and inhaled the morning air. Eh, what, he thought, life is still beautiful. Then he put on his pants and shoes. In the kitchen, he cut himself a slice of bread, and from the corner, he took the fishing rod and the old can and left the house.

He set out over the rugged cobbles of the town square, and the pavement seemed to resonate under his heavy, manly steps. He walked around the church. He, however, did not turn left on the uphill road towards the vineyards, where he saw farmers in the distance. Instead, he chose the narrow way on the right that led around the fields down towards the river.

In the distance before him, he saw three men. He quickened his pace, and as he was getting near, he recognized them. The first one who bestrode the unsaddled horse was young Klvaňa. Okáník was swaying next to him. Behind them walked ailing Palo Markovič. Today was a Sunday, but the fields were calling, and it was necessary to pointlessly plow in the sowing and weed the last beets and potatoes. Jacob caught up with them, wished them good morning, and opened a conversation with them.

"Going fishing? Going fishing?" Klvaňa bared his white teeth while sitting on his horse.

"They could take the bait today," thought old Okáník.

"We will have nothing else to eat soon anyway," countered Klvaňa and spat in a wide arc.

"That's it, that's it," nodded Okáník. "We will die, we will die, like hungry dogs we will die."

"And what about the vineyards?" asked Jacob.

Okáník just waved his hand with sadness and angrily cursed through clenched teeth: "To hell with them. They are lost. What we saved is not worth a hoot."

"We will perish. We will perish like dogs," continued Okáník.

Only Markovič was quiet. From time to time, he just moved the heavy hoe from shoulder to shoulder, and his ailing body seemed to be even more miserable than Klvaňa's rage and the old man's wailing.

At the white chapel with the faded picture of the Virgin Mary, decorated with a dried bunch of bluebottles, Okáník made the sign of the cross. Klvaňa just cussed some inarticulate words and kicked the horse hard so that he jumped up.

Here Jacob said goodbye to the men as their way continued further to their little fields, whereas he followed a pathway turning to the right towards the river.

The air, warmed up by weeks of sultry weather, already smelled of water, and the closer he was getting to the river, it also smelled of fish. The footpath led right up to the river and then wound around the shore of the lazy flow. The silence embracing the morning landscape was interrupted only by the oscillations of the transparent wings of swift dragonflies. Here and there, a fish rose above the heated-up surface and then fell back inside the water with a loud smack. The circles on the surface spread after each smack to both shores, to the left one, where Jacob walked, and also to the right, covered in brushwood, and their trembling wobbled the shadows of trees and bushes. In the reeds before the river's curve, a kingfisher sat down and swung on the elastic stalk. Jacob stopped in order to not disturb him. But the bird chirped twice and flew towards the brushwood on the other side of the river.

Jacob went a little bit further and stopped at a place where the river made a sharp turn. He walked to the water's edge, put his fishing rod and can on the ground, checked his fishing line, and skillfully attached the worm to the hook. Then he again grabbed the rod and swung the fishing line in a wide arch into the middle of the river. He stood for a while and held the rod in his hand while watching it float motionlessly on the surface. Then he drove the end of the rod into the bank, weighed it down with the nearby stone, and sat down on the shore. He then embraced his knees with his hands and gazed into the water.

In spite of all, life is still beautiful, Jacob said to himself in the morning when he woke up. But he could not stop thinking about Rebecca. Other times, when he sat on the bank and waited till the motionless float made a jerky movement on the surface before it suddenly submerged, he did not think about anything else besides the catch. There were no happier hours for him than those spent with the fishing rod at the riverbank or with the birds in the forest. Jacob was at home in nature. The peace his father was searching for through the dialog with the Lord was found by him in the silence of the forests, in the whispering of the breeze in the reeds, in the quiet flight of the birds high above the river. But today, he felt bitter, and his heart was shadowed.

Never before did he so deeply realize the emptiness of what was between him and Rebecca as today. Rebecca walked around the house without a smile, she did not want to be hugged, and in her every word, there was something sour. She did not know how to enjoy trivial things with Jacob. She did not try to go with him to the fields and did not attempt to listen to the language of the birds. She just sat at home all the time and complained to Theresa that Jacob did not help her with anything and at the same time tried to set Jacob against his mother. Jacob never got mad but thought that it was pretty silly. In the evening, when he returned home after his work, he hoped to hear a nice word and to feel a soft palm. But Rebecca tried to avoid his embrace and did not talk about anything else other than the worries bearing down on them, as if Jacob himself did not hear enough about them.

And it will stay like that, he thought. He felt ashamed to acknowledge that his father was right. But now that they are expecting a child, it is too late. Nothing will change. It will be the same forever.

The float made several jerky movements on the surface, and Jacob grabbed the rod. But the float did not submerge, and when

Jacob inspected the fishing line, he saw that the fish just bit the worm off and swam away. He put some new bait on the hook and swung the fishing line again in a wide arc into the middle of the river.

At that moment, a small boat appeared at the curve of the stream. The oars, set in rusty swivels, squeaked at every stroke. The woman sitting at the oars had her back turned towards Jacob. She wore a light blue summer dress with short sleeves, and her bare suntanned arms stroked the paddles somewhat clumsily and dipped them unnecessarily deep. The loose clothes briefly uncovered her left shoulder, and her movements revealed her body's soft elasticity. But Jacob did not pay any attention to all of that. He just angrily hissed as the squeaky noises and the rippled surface frightened off the fish. He reeled in the fishing line and got ready to move around the bank away from the boat to some quieter place. The squeaking of the oars, however, suddenly stopped, and he heard a joyful voice coming from the ship:

"Jacob!"

He paused and shaded his eyes with his hand.

"Is it you, Jacob?" sounded again from the boat that turned around and was nearing the shore with renewed squeaking of the oars. He now recognized the woman and called out in surprise:

"Helen!"

The boat reached the shore, and Helen, with a happy smile on her glowing face, tried to get out of the unsteady dinghy fast. When she stepped out onto the bank, she stumbled across the chain at the stern of the boat and would have fallen if Jacob had not caught her. For a moment, for less than a second, they stood in an embrace. For a moment, he felt her bosom but quickly backed off.

"Miss Helen, what a surprise. What are you doing here?" he asked confusedly.

"Since when am I a miss?" she smiled into his face.

"Helen, from where have you fallen here?" he corrected himself.

"That is better," she continued to smile. "I am spending my vacation here. My uncle left me a cottage up in the vineyards, and I want to rest here for a while."

Jacob pulled the dinghy's stern onto the shore, and they sat next to each other on the ground. He recalled that he heard about the death of Helen's uncle, pastor Garaj. While alive, he used to be a cheerful fellow with cheeks red from the wine for which he had a passion. People gossiped that women did not come to see him just for a confession. There was also a rumor that Helen was, in fact, his daughter. Her mother, whom Jacob did not remember but who was said to be very pretty, died during childbirth. And three years later, her father, who belonged among the wealthy farmers, was killed by a runaway horse. Once he died, pastor Garaj took his brother's child under his care, and Helen grew up in the rectory. That's probably why the myth about the pastor's paternity was created. But it was clear that pastor Garaj took truly fatherly care of Helen and provided for her even after his death.

Jacob knew Helen since they were little children. Pastor Garaj was an unusual priest. People liked him and could not hold anything against him as he spoke their simple language. He was not even scared to use some crude, profane words from the pulpit. He played cards with Aaron Timfeld and brush-maker Tolnai, and he did not prevent Helen from becoming friends with Jewish children. The rectory was not far from Gabriel Menasse's house, and so Helen used to come to play with Jacob and his brothers. Even other children from the neighborhood gathered in the storage room of Gabriel's malting house and spent happy moments filled with childish games there.

Jacob and Helen, who had not seen each other in years, recalled those happy times now.

"And do you recall furfang?" Jacob interrupted Helen's speech.

"Furfang bang?"

"Furfang bang," clapped Jacob on his knees.

Furfang was the nickname for a big cistern cart from which they drew beer into the barrels in the brewery. Children heard that word for the first time from the warehouse keeper Němec and never used a different name for it afterward. Once, they played in Gabriel's storage room where they drew the beer. Jacob sat on a sack for barley and held in his hand a large weight and pretended that it was a cistern or a furfang. Helen held a straw and pretended that it was a hose through which the beer was drawn into smaller weights representing barrels. The heavy weight slipped from Jacob's hand and fell on little Helen's head. At that time, Helen was not yet able to talk well. She just started to cry, and when they asked her what had happened to her, she only repeated: "Furfang bang, furfang bang!"

"I still have a scar," she laughed. "Look at it!"

She pulled apart the dark brown hair covering her forehead, and Jacob leaned towards her to see it. For the second time, he was so close to her that he smelled the scent of her skin. Helen raised her head, and for a moment, her forehead touched his cheek. Jacob felt the warmth of her touch and moved quickly away from her. To hide his embarrassment, he grabbed an already almost forgotten fishing rod from the ground, got up, attached a new bait, and threw the line into the river. Then he drove the end of the rod again into the bank and again weighed it down with a boulder. But as soon as he did that and was getting ready to sit down next to Helen, the float that appeared for a few moments motionless on the surface suddenly swiftly submerged. Jacob just managed to catch the rod bent under the weight of the caught fish. He quickly pulled it out. At the end of the fishing line, quite a large carp was tossing around. Jacob skillfully removed the fishhook and placed his catch into the can filled with the water from the river.

Jacob's self-confident movements and his steadiness surprised Helen.

"You see," she laughed, "you sit here for a while and do not catch anything. And then, when you least expect it, the catch falls right into your lap."

"It was you who brought me good luck," he turned to her while smiling and swung the fishing line again into the middle of the river.

"What's up with you? You alone are not lucky enough?" she asked.

Jacob did not answer, but his shining face became suddenly more serious. Helen's question meant just as a joke, rang in his ears. You alone are not lucky enough? You are not lucky enough? You are not lucky? He heard that question again and again, and it reverberated like an echo. The dull emptiness of his life with Rebecca, which was forgotten for a few moments, stood clearly before him.

Helen noticed a sudden change in Jacob's face but did not say anything. After a while, she got up. They stood now next to each other, Jacob with the rod in his hand, Helen shading eyes from sunlight with her palm, and they both looked silently at the water. As the float twice made a jerky movement on the surface, Helen got excited and put her hand on Jacob's shoulder. But she kept it there even after the float quieted down. This time, Jacob did not try to get away.

After a moment, while still looking at the quiet surface, she asked him directly:

"Jacob, are you happy?"

It took a while for him to reply. But then he said:

"Yes. I am married. We are expecting a child."

Then he pulled the fishing line out so that he could replace the bait. Helen took her hand down from his shoulder.

"I am glad to hear it," she said. And after a moment, she added: "So I will go. Have a nice time here, fisherman."

"I will help you put the boat back on the water."

"No, thank you, I will leave the boat here. I will come back up to the vineyard on this way across the field."

"In that case, I will accompany you for a moment."

Jacob pulled the dinghy's stern even more up on the bank and placed a large stone weight on the chain. Then he threw the rod over his shoulder, gathered the can with the caught carp, and they set out on a journey back home through the path between the parched fields.

They did not talk much. Only once they reached the chapel where they parted ways did Helen say:

"I am sure we will still meet again."

"I am sure."

"I will stay in the cottage for about a month."

"I am sure we will see each other before you leave."

He smiled at her one more time, waved goodbye to her, and stepped out on the field road down to the town. After a few steps, he turned around. Helen turned around at the same time.

"Have a nice time, fisherman," she called to Jacob and started to run on the road leading up to the vineyards.

He waved at her with the hand holding the rod. Then he again turned and continued in his way. He felt somewhat lighter.

Chapter 8

Helen

Jacob's contentment that had arisen from meeting Helen, however, did not last long. It disappeared once he woke up the following day by Rebecca's side. And as, after the dried-out spring, there is a jagged hole in the ground resembling an open wound, so the lost contentment left a painful scar on Jacob's heart. A few happy moments spent with Helen and focused on his childhood memories would not get out of his mind. He recalled them again and again in his spirit, and they were gradually more and more transforming into a picture of a green oasis in his joyless life. It is nonsense, he was saying to himself.

Everything is just nonsense. I will get over it, he was trying to push his uneasiness away. I am again on a journey through the desert.

But the spring of living water that he had just tasted was still nearby. Why not come back? Why not get only a sip to moisten his parched lips? He could not wipe out of his memories the moment when he caught Helen as she was exiting the boat and when he felt her firm breasts on his chest, and a moment when her forehead touched his cheek. He was overcome with fear.

Jacob was not a saint. When he was still single, it was easy for him to grab girls from the fields and into the woods and to make love with them on some warmed-up moss in hidden clearings of the forest. And during his military service, he even slept with Gipsy girls. But since he married Rebecca three years ago, he has not touched another woman.

All his life changed that day, and Rebecca's coldness, which became apparent soon after their wedding, broke even his passion into a resigned ordinariness. But those brief moments when he had touched Helen's youthful body fanned a smoldering spark in him, and Jacob realized with fear how close the fire was, which threatened to engulf him.

For two days, he was able to resist. He attended morning and evening synagogue services with his father and devoted all the time in between to work and was hardly leaving the malting house. But on the third morning, he went again to the river. At the stream curve, where he met Helen, he found Helen's dinghy as they left it there, with the stern pulled up far on the bank and with the chain weighted down by the large stone.

But he did not find what he was looking for.

The next day he was able to control himself.

But the day after, he took his fishing rod and the can again, crossed the town square, and made a turn on the field road leading to the river. He started to walk faster once he was on the trail leading from the crossing at the chapel to the shore. He rushed to the curve in the stream and found the dinghy at its old place. But the boat, pulled entirely out of the water, was turned over with its bottom facing up.

Jacob attached the bait to the fishhook. He was ashamed of his hands as they appeared to be shaky now. Then he swung the line in a high arc into the water. But he had to take it out right away as the hook did not end up far from the bank and lashed it out once more. Then he drove the end of the rod into the bank, sat down on the bottom of Helen's boat, and looked at the water.

Then it suddenly crossed his mind that the turned-over dinghy on which he was sitting had to have some meaning. Helen had to be here yesterday and had to pull the boat on the bank. What else could it mean then that she was getting ready to leave? She told him that she would stay for the entire month, but women can change their minds really easily. He got confused. Helen departed, and he will not see her anymore. It was not until now that he realized how much he wanted to have her. For a moment, he felt relieved. He jumped off the dinghy, his shaky hands grabbed the fishing rod and the can, and he started to run on the pathway to the road leading up to the vineyards.

Helen's cottage, inherited from her uncle, pastor Garaj, was at the end of the row of wooden one-story buildings, covered with white and blue plaster and standing right on the foot of a slope with vineyards. Her uncle used to hide there for his meditations but also for heroic drinking sprees with his friends. The cottage was uninhabited since the priest's death. Helen spent a lot of time cleaning it from the cobwebs that covered the kitchenette and the main room in the hut.

News about her inheritance reached Helen on the day of her birthday – she was again one year older and still unmarried – and it mentioned that she had inherited from her uncle not only the cottage but also some money that the priest saved during his life. And that message was of crucial importance for Helen.

She was twenty-seven years old and worked as a middle school teacher in Trnava. But she did not like the teaching as, since her childhood, she dreamed about joining the theater. Already as a little girl, she loved to change into various clothes or make disguises. From old sacks in Menasse's storage, she made a trail and showed Jacob how the queen walked or how the old Gabaňa woman limped. At the school in Nitra, she played in an amateur theater, and it was the first and only time in her life that she fell in love. A young teacher Lukáč who used to play lovers had deep-seated black eyes and a captivating voice that stole Helen's heart. They met in secret but soon after losing her virginity, she also lost her lover as he died suddenly from pneumonia. Since that time, except for a few short-lived showers, she was not in love with anybody. Since that time, she dreamed only about theater. While examining her students in tributaries of the Danube on the left, while correcting their stylistic essays, and while sitting behind the desk in her classroom, she thought about theater. Only there, on the stage, could she genuinely live.

Teaching was only a source of income for her. While she took part in some amateur theater, Professor Rohan from the conservatory who was visiting his sister noticed her. After the performance, he approached Helen in the changing room and told her:

"Listen to me, my girl. You've got some talent. You should study. In a year or two, I could make something out of you. Would you be interested?"

Why should she not be interested? But could she afford it? How would she support herself? Her uncle was very nice to her, but he did not want to hear a word about the theater. So Helen had to stay in her classroom at Trnava's middle school with her deep longing.

But the inheritance from her uncle changed everything. Helen decided to leave school and become an actress. Pastor Garaj, however, passed sometime in June, and at that time of year, it was not possible to join the theater. Helen was thus glad that she could get some rest in the brick cottage and get ready for acting auditions awaiting her after the summer break.

She wrote a letter to Rohan, but he did not reply. She nevertheless hoped that some theater company would accept her for the coming fall and the money inherited from her uncle would secure her financially in case the search for a contract would last longer. She brought with her several plays, and while walking across the room in the hut, she played for days Juliet and Desdemona, Roxanne and Joan of Arc.

At that moment, she stood next to the window on the south side of the house. Strong stalks of sunflowers were leaning towards it, and one could see across them far into the countryside. She rested on the windowsill and looked at the freshly plowed fields. Then she pressed her hands against her bosom and was again Juliet on the balcony talking to invisible Romeo somewhere down on the dusty road in front of the cottage.

"O Romeo," she wept into the open space where there was not a living soul.

"Romeo! Wherefore art thou Romeo?
Deny thy father and refuse thy name.
Or, if thou wilt not, be but sworn my love,
And I'll no longer be a Capulet."

Suddenly, she overheard hurried steps. She leaned out of the window and recognized Jacob, rushing towards her, with the rod across his shoulder and the can in his hand.

"Hello, fisherman!" she called with a smile as he got closer.

He stopped under the window, and his face brightened.

"I thought that you already left," he said shyly.

"Left? And why?"

"I saw the dinghy pulled up on the bank."

"Oh, I see," she laughed. "I pulled it up yesterday and turned it upside down. It has to start raining one day. I was afraid that it would float away."

They kept silent for a moment. Then Jacob said:

"I am glad that you have not left yet." Then he got more serious and added: "I had to see you again."

"I am glad that you came," she tried to help him, and with a smile in her voice, she suggested: "Don't you want to drink some wine, fisherman?"

She ran outside to him. She walked barefooted and had on her only a light sleeveless dress decorated with flowers, revealing rather than hiding the charms of her body. Her loose dark hair fell on naked, round, and tanned shoulders.

The room into which Jacob entered was half-filled with sunlight next to the window. In the other half, sunbeams had no access. The shade border was in the center of the room, where an old oak table with four chairs with knitted backrests stood. On the table, there was a glass jug with wildflowers, an ink bottle with a pen leaning on the plug, and several books. In the darkened half of the room, there was a large, carved wardrobe in one corner, and in the other one, a sofa, covered with a dark red blanket and a cushion from a pink eiderdown cover. Above the couch, large photographs of pastor Garaj and his parents hung in black frames.

Helen took the rod and the can from Jacob's hand, put them in the corner behind the wardrobe, and popped out to the kitchen. After a while, she got back with a flagon of the wine and two glasses. She filled the glasses with the red sourness, and they drank a toast.

"To your health, fisherman."

"To your health, Helen."

They smiled at each other with their eyes over the edge of the glasses. They were again for a moment playful like children, like during their first meeting. Once they finished up, they placed the empty glasses on the table, and Helen filled them up again.

"Do you recall princess Genevieve?" she laughed.

"That one with a trail from the sack?"

"Why do you insult my royal gown, prince Hadraban?"

The room was filled with her ringing laughter. Jacob saw how the smile flowed through her body like a stream. As she tilted her head back, her bosom seemed to dance under the thin dress.

He did not smile. This time, he did not get infected with Helen's unbridled optimism. Once her eyes, filled with tears from her laughter, met Jacob's solemn face again, she immediately calmed down.

He hugged her, and while his shaky hands held her waist, he pulled her down to himself. Then he passionately kissed her. She only apprehensively whispered: "Jacob!" He embraced her even more firmly and kissed her again. When she reciprocated his kiss, Jacob felt dizzy. He hugged her with his entire body. She did not try to pull away from him even after he grabbed her glowing cheeks into his palms like a large, sweet fruit and kissed her voraciously. He felt how she stroked his back and fondled his hair and placed his own hand on her breasts. She trembled under his warm palms but did not resist.

With feverish haste, they ripped off their clothes, and in an embrace of tangled arms, they fell on the sofa, heavily like two wrestlers.

Once they finally wearied after the bout of pleasure, they felt how the emptied bliss filled their hearts with pity. They laid down quietly next to each other, Jacob's eyes roved about the ceiling, and Helen pretended to sleep. She then started to talk.

"What will we do, Jacob?" she whispered.

He did not tear his eyes away from the ceiling, only his hand on which Helen's head was resting embraced her shoulder tenderly, and he did not answer for a while. Then he said:

"I will leave with you." In his voice, certainty mingled with sadness.

"You cannot do that, Jacob," she told him anxiously. "You have a wife, and you will have a child." She cuddled up under Jacob's arm and started to weep.

"I will leave with you," Jacob repeated. "We will run away. Away! Away from here."

"We cannot, Jacob, we cannot," she started to sob loudly. "We should not see each other again. Never again."

He turned to her, embraced her in his arms, and between kisses whispered:

"I have to. I have to have you. I am suffocating here. I will choke. I will perish."

He wept bitter tears into her hair. She clasped his head to her warm bosom and stroked his face as a mother trying to soothe a little boy who woke up from a bad dream.

Thus they laid down in silence for a long time in a quiet embrace. Heavy drops of water falling on the windows later interrupted their peace. After many months, it started to rain.

"I have to go," Jacob got up and put on his clothes in haste.

"You will get wet," Helen mounted a weak defense.

"I have to go," he repeated in a firmer tone and tightened his belt. He resembled a soldier getting ready for the battlefield.

He bent once more to Helen and kissed her on the forehead. Then he grabbed the rod and the can and ran out of the house.

Once he was on the road covered with a layer of dust

perforated by the first heavy drops of rain, he could hear her call coming from the window.

"Jacob!"

Helen stood next to the window wrapped in a sofa cover, and her voice trembled.

"Come soon, Jacob," she begged him in a half-whisper. "Don't leave me here alone for long."

Jacob stopped and looked for a long time into Helen's face and saw her tears slowly trickling down.

"I will come," he finally uttered from his tight throat and then quickly turned around and started to run on the road down to the town. The rain was getting thicker and soaked his clothes. But Jacob did not feel its wet coldness. He thought about a different rain. The rain that fell to irrigate the sands of his desert, the rain which cannot stop and which will never stop. He made his decision.

Chapter 9

Game of Cards

When the weather was not good enough for taking a stroll through Creekside Street up to the Small Grove, Gabriel Menasse spent his Sunday afternoons at Philip's place. They played together with baker Spitzer a kreuzer mariáš. Kreuzer, in fact, only while they still had kreuzers. Nowadays, they only recorded a detailed account of their debts which they did not pay.

Since the day when the rain started, the skies did not smile. The downpour lasted only a day, and except for some late beets, it did not save any more crops. But it brought with it a sudden wave of cold weather, the skies remained covered with heavy and dark clouds, and bouts of strong wind were breaking branches from dried up trees. It was not a time for strolls. And so, even this Sunday, Gabriel came to Philip's house. Spitzer was already waiting there. He seemed to become sadder from day to day as Ferenčák did not bring a letter from his son in America.

Chana made coffee, poured it into large green cups with golden rims inherited from her deceased mother, and brought it to the old men into the room next to Philip's workshop. She also baked ginger pastries. Poverty could be around everywhere, but ginger pastries made from the dough using a special pastry cutter in the shape of crenelations were never in short supply in Chana's house. Without them, the actual end would be for sure near.

When playing cards, the old men seemed to be young again. Philip smiled regardless of whether he was winning or losing. But Spitzer did not take defeats lightly, and when losing, he fell deeper and deeper into his sadness. Gabriel shone whenever he was dealt good cards. However, he boiled with rage when losing and would angrily blame his rivals and would argue with them as well as with himself.

That afternoon, however, the luck smiled at Gabriel, and in the accounts kept by Philip, his numbers were rising. He was a dealer again. He exchanged with some hesitation his talon and his bearded face gleamed as he announced:

"So I would have one hundred seven in acorns."

Baker Spitzer looked at his cards and unhappily shook his head. But smiling Philip countered:

"Good."

"So good again," called Gabriel, and his fist pounded on the table.

"Fine, show us what you have."

Gabriel pondered for a while, then played a green ace, and said:

"Let's start in the forest."

"Woods are green," said Spitzer, indicating that he was following suit.

"But they cut the trees down," smiled Philip and took Gabriel's ace with a trump eight.

Gabriel still made his hundred, but Philip caught his announced seven.

"How could I know that you had no greens?" he was annoyed with Philip. "And why do you put on such a solemn face when you are blessed with such good cards?" he turned angrily to Spitzer. "Without your tortured appearance, I would never redouble." Then he chewed the tip of his beard in a huff.

At that moment, it was possible to hear the voices behind the door, and Chana ushered Aaron Timfeld into the room. His bright face greeted them with a wide smile.

"What a special guest we have," called Philip and asked Chana to bring another chair as he raised his eyes from the card game. "Mr. Rosh Hakol! What a special guest we have."

"I was just walking around and decided to say hello," Timfeld said as an excuse. He sat down on a wide chair next to Philip and asked: "So, how is the game?"

"Just as you walked in, I became bedeviled by bad luck," replied half-jokingly Gabriel, whose fortune really had reversed.

Philip smiled aside at Timfeld, who understood that Gabriel was having one of his bad moments again and, for that reason, was simply looking at Philip's cards without saying a word. Every once in a while, he also checked Spitzer's hand as he also sat next to him. He belonged to those kibitzers who do not advise and feel satisfied by knowing more about the cards in the game than those playing at the table. He thanked Chana for the coffee, praised her ginger pastries, and quietly listened as the cards hit the desk.

Baker Spitzer won the next game, and Timfeld watched what Philip recorded in his columns.

"It's so much money," he smiled. "If the kehilla had so much, my hair would not be so white."

"Why don't you play? You could win some money for the kehilla's expenses." Spitzer's face was shining for a moment as he was proud of his joke.

But Gabriel shouted angrily: "Those are bad jokes!" He then gave Spitzer a piercing stare, and the baker curled up and resumed his timid sadness.

"No matter whether those ideas are good or bad," Timfeld tried to seize the opportunity to talk about the reason why he came, as all of them knew anyway that he did not stop by just to greet them. "One thing is clear. We have to do something. Days go by, and we have not come up with any smart solution. I cannot handle it anymore," he added after a pause.

Gabriel looked at Philip and Spitzer as they sat around while holding the cards but not focusing on the game. He then turned his own cards upside down, put them on the table, and asked Timfeld directly:

"And what should we do?"

Timfeld shrugged his broad shoulders and then slowly and carefully measured every word:

"I have thought a lot about Kantůrek's suggestion."

Philip leaned on the backrest of the chair and clasped a fan of cards to his chest. Baker Spitzer was nodding. Only Gabriel's eyes radiated angry tension. Timfeld looked at all three and checked what reactions were generated by his words. Then he continued:

"I was mad as much as you were," he said, and Gabriel's face became recognizably more relaxed. "I also did not like it. That is clear. I did not like it at all. And I do not like it even now."

He paused for a while and studied their faces. But then, as if he suddenly made his decision, he started to proclaim:

"What other options do we have? In the end, the same thing will happen. Those things will just move from our shul to another."

"Those things! Those things!" Gabriel attacked him, and Timfeld quickly tried to gloss over those unwisely chosen words.

"To whom else could Braun from Břeclav sell our Holy Torahs than to some other kehilla that still has some money?" And he tried to emphasize the word "Holy" to placate Gabriel. But Gabriel just muttered into his beard:

"The Torahs and the Mizrachs are not for sale." But his voice did not sound as upset as before, and Timfeld mustered up the courage for the next step.

"Do you think," he said and looked at the others as if he really sought their advice. "Do you think that it would be too bad if we just invited Braun? He could look at what we have and tell us the value of everything. We will at least know, financially, the possibilities. What do you think?"

They remained silent for a moment. Then the baker sat up in his chair and timidly proposed:

"I think we could ask." And when he saw that nobody opposed him, he added: "That does not cost us anything."

Philip just shrugged his shoulders and, with a downcast gaze, pretended to focus on his cards. Gabriel again looked at the fan, which he still pressed with his hairy hand to the table. Those eyes under his thick eyebrows secretly roamed from Philip to Spitzer, and once he realized that he was alone, his fist pounded on the table:

"So, do we play, or do we just waffle?" And he played the card and channeled all his anger and helplessness into the smack of the card on the table. "Diamonds," he announced in a half-broken voice.

Spitzer began to nod again and played a jack. Philip then did not take Gabriel's card even though he was able to.

Chapter 10

David

Daniel did not like those games. They were silly and perhaps only suitable for girls. But David was persistent, and there was not a lot of fun with him anyway, so what else should he do?

He was a weird boy, this Cousin David, and Daniel could never fully understand him. His freckled nose and shortsighted eyes with glasses were constantly only stuck in books. He was more careful than anybody else to not eat meat dishes from dairy plates and vice versa. He was anxious to make sure that he never forgot to say the correct blessing appropriate for each occasion. Underneath his shirt, he wore tzitzit, its fringes visibly hanging out. And he always hastened to be at home before the first star appeared in the skies. It happened one Friday evening that their maid Barbara forgot to come to David's room to put out his paraffin lamp. He could not put it out by himself as Shabbat started already with the first star in the sky, and that is why he decided to go to sleep and keep the light on. However, when he was putting on a nightgown, the movement of his arm accidentally extinguished the flame. David spent that night crying and praying, and he fasted for the entire day afterward. He was a weird boy. It was pretty difficult to convince him to participate in any game. And though Daniel did not like those girlish activities, he finally accepted David's proposal to play heaven-inferno-paradise.

He drew a giant horseshoe on the sidewalk in front of Grandfather Gabriel's house using chalk. He then extended it with two long lines and connected them at the end. Then he traced a long line in the horseshoe center and finally separated the entire field into eight equal squares. In the last square on the left, he wrote a big letter H for heaven, in the last one on the right I for inferno, and in the oval end of the horseshoe, he drew a nice large P. It was for paradise. Then they found two large chips of glass, a brown one from a beer bottle for Daniel and a white one from a mug, which Barbara broke while doing dishes, for David. Daniel proudly inspected his drawing and then placed the chip on the toes of his barefoot and jumped carefully from square to square, so that the chip would not fall off and he would not touch the lines separating the fields.

Then he suddenly stopped, and while still standing on one foot, he turned his head towards David:

"David, guess what. Do you think heaven, inferno or hell, and paradise really exist?"

David was just trying to attach the white glass chip to his leg so that it would hold as firmly as possible. When he heard Daniel's question, he straightened up, and as if he did not understand that somebody could have any doubts about it, he frowned up his forehead in surprise and said:

"Of course, heaven exists."

"And hell?"

"Hell exists as well."

"And paradise?"

"Of course."

Those nearsighted eyes behind his glasses that timidly fluttered with the anxiety caused by Daniel's queries were suggestive of doubts. Daniel jumped over another line, but he stopped again and probingly looked at David before making another move.

"And you believe that?"

"And you don't?"

On David's pale forehead, one could see even more wrinkles now. Daniel did not respond but carelessly stepped, on purpose, and the chip fell off his leg. He hissed as if he were mad at himself for such clumsiness and said:

"It's your turn now."

David placed his chip on his instep and lifted up his leg, getting ready for the first jump. He jumped into the first square, jumped over the second line but was too distracted to hold his leg steady. The white chip bounced on the pavement, and it was Daniel's turn again. Daniel threw his chip at the wall at that moment, and it shattered into thousands of pieces. Then he announced:

"I hate it, I really hate it. I do not play anymore."

"So, what will we do?" David asked surprised.

"I am going home."

"Don't go. What will you do at home?" David tried to persuade him.

And he was right. He could not play any exciting games with David, and he was weird, but Jura Tomík, who was probably in front of their house right now, was even dumber.

"Do you know what?" he got an idea. "Let's go to check the mulberries."

"OK, let's go." David threw away his chip too, and off they went.

Grandfather Philip owned a small field up the hill behind the vineyards. He never tended it by himself, and for a few crowns per year and some potatoes, he rented it for years already to the neighbor Gabaňa. But on the edge of the field, several grown trees and their fruit still belonged to Philip. There were almost no apples on the apple trees this summer, and the pears were crawling with maggots to the point that it made no sense to try to cut them out. But there were also three mulberry trees there, and the boys started to crave the insipid taste of their sweet fruits.

They set out on the journey up to the vineyards. They followed the rutted cart track around the fields and had nothing to talk about for a while. Daniel whistled, and with a wooden stick, he beat the grass blades in the dried-up ditch next to the path. And David dragged behind him a sizeable dry branch that left a line in the high dust of the road. On the trail, there was a dead frog.

Daniel picked it up and swung it in front of David's nose.

"Here is roast meat for you," he laughed wildly, "and do not forget to recite your blessing for meat."

David shuddered in disgust and started to run.

"Why don't you leave me alone?" he begged almost tearfully when Daniel reached him.

"Because you are a dumb boy who believes everything."

"What do I believe?" protested David.

"Everything. That there is hell and paradise and that there are angels and demons."

"And you do not believe that?" David asked again with surprise like the first time.

"Of course I don't," said Daniel. "Those are just fairy tales for little children." One could hear the disdain in his voice. He bent down and picked up a stag beetle from the ground as he saw its wings shining in the sunlight. He then hid it in a matchbox that he found in his pocket.

"Why bother with hell?" he continued contemptuously. "In the end, you also believe that the shepherd Ivanko sold his soul to the devil, don't you?"

"I do believe," David admitted defiantly and slammed the ground with his branch so that the dust swirled around.

"I could have thought that. Just so you know, you wiseacre, Ivanko is no demon, just a poor man. Do you hear me? Just a poor man. Some comedian stole his wife, and he thus became a drunkard and a mad man."

"How do you know?" David wondered.

"I know it, and that's the end of it. If you want to know something, there is no hell and no demons as well."

"And what about paradise?"

"When there is no hell, then there is no paradise. That's common sense."

"So tell me what exists," David went on the offensive.

"Nothing, so you would know, absolutely nothing. There are only bad people hurting the good ones."

Daniel stepped on a hairy caterpillar that was crawling through the dust to the ditch and remained silent. Why try to explain all those things to the dumb boy? He will not change him anyway, and he himself will not make any progress either. He cut a grass blade with the stick and quickened his pace. But David, pattering next to him, used a moment of silence to carefully contemplate everything Daniel said. Finally, he attacked Daniel with winning certainty:

"But even if you were right and there was no paradise and no hell, there would still be heaven, and in heaven, there is a God, and he punishes bad people."

"Oh yeah? Punishes and punishes," Daniel ridiculed while laughing loudly, but then he suddenly exploded: "He does not punish, and that is the problem!"

"He does punish," insisted David. "Grandpa told me that he does."

"Grandpa told me, Grandpa told me," Daniel mimicked his voice. "Grandpa must know everything."

"He truly punishes. I am sure you also overheard how Grandpa told Uncle Jacob that God would punish those who did not fear him."

Nothing could bend David's confidence. But Daniel just grinned:

"Grandpa said so. So that you would know that there was no reason for Grandpa to get mad because Uncle Jacob is not a bad man."

"He is bad. He does not go to shul."

"He is not. He never hurts anybody. He does not even beat the horses."

"But he does not pray, and Grandpa said that through his impiety, he inflicts God's wrath on all of us. Yes, that is how he explained it. You had to hear it too."

"And you also believe that?"

"I do. I do believe it," David stood his ground and again slammed the dust of the road with his branch.

"Let's stop. Why should I argue with you?" Daniel ended the conversation. He then tore a leaf of burdock in the ditch and put a piece of it into the matchbox with the stag beetle.

They thus reached the first vineyards and then walked on the path that led around cottages with white and blue plaster towards Philip's field with mulberry trees. The sun was shining on the vineyard hills, but nobody worked at them now as the poor harvest was already over, and the farmers simply waited for whether the blight would die down when there were no more grapes on the bushes. Every once in a while, they came to check on the vineyards, burned down the affected bushes, and hoed the soil around the remaining ones. But they would always come back home with their hope further diminished.

Once they reached the end of the row of cottages, they caught sight of the round yellow cakes of sunflowers whose stiff, strong blades flanked the windows of the last building. Without thinking twice, they ran across the pathway from the ditch to the house and started to extract sunflower plant seeds. They gathered them into their mouths as well as pockets and spat the dry peels on the road in front of the window. The unexpected harvest made them happy, and they forgot that a few moments ago, they had almost engaged in a fight over heaven, hell, and paradise.

Daniel got the idea to look into the closed window under which they stood. He suddenly felt that his heart was pounding somewhere up in his throat. He pulled David abruptly close to himself, put his hand on his mouth, crouched so that only his forehead and eyes were above the windowsill, and held his breath. David also hunched so that only his eyes reached the frame and trembled with terrible fear once he looked inside. His teeth, covered by Daniel's hot hand, started to chatter.

On the couch in the darkened back half of the room where sunlight did not reach, laid a man and a woman. The nakedness of their bodies, embracing each other, reflected in the dark background of the room. They laid there with their limbs intertwined, connected in an undulating and passionately moving bundle. The boys recognized Jacob hugging an unfamiliar woman. They could not hear the liberating sighs of the lovers through the closed window, but the silence further magnified the horror in the rapidly thumping hearts of David and Daniel. They could not remove their eyes off this pantomime, cruel and horridly beautiful at the same time. Beautiful as the drawing back of a curtain that was until now hiding a secret. And cruel through the witnessing of the sin that was throbbing in their temples while repeating an eternal echo: "Uncle Jacob, Jacob, Ja-cob!"

They were both trembling with excitement. Suddenly, on his hand that was covering David's mouth, Daniel felt a droplet flowing down. He looked at David. From his terrified eyes, heavy tears trickled quietly down while he arduously tried to hide his sobbing. Daniel became frightened, pulled David quickly away from the window and onto the road, and then dragged him hastily through the dust of the path away from the building.

They had long forgotten about the mulberries and ran back on the same path that had taken them there. David's sobbing gradually became louder.

"You see that he is evil," he was moaning. "I knew that he was evil."

Then Daniel suddenly stopped, and while he was still holding David's hand, he yelled into his face:

"You have not seen anything. Do you hear me? You will not say a word to anybody. Not a word. That's their business. Do you understand?"

David was simply sobbing silently and was spreading the tears with his dirty hands, which were sweating from excitement, all over his face.

"Have you heard? Not a word about this to anyone," Daniel repeated even more forcefully.

"One peep and I will beat you up." And then he suddenly squeezed David's hand so that it hurt and ordered him: "Swear that you will not say a word to anybody."

"I cannot. I am not allowed to," David sobbed even louder than before.

"I am telling you – swear!"

"I am not allowed to. I will not tell anybody, but I am not allowed to swear," David moaned bitterly.

"Swear!" yelled Daniel. But David suddenly, with unexpected force, slipped away and started to run through the hot dust of the roadway.

Daniel initially wanted to run after him, but then just waved his hand and sluggishly dragged himself towards home. He sat down on the first milestone and held his face in his palms while supporting his elbows on his knees. His head was spinning.

He did not know for how long he sat there. He finally jumped up from the milestone, stood up, and with solemn steps – as if not boyish anymore – continued on his journey. After a while, he grabbed the box with the stag beetle from his pocket, took it out, and threw it in a wide arc into the fields around the road.

Chapter 11

Mother

The afternoon sun was still warmly shining upon Theresa's white hair and her lap where she held her sewing. She sat next to the window on a kitchen chair as she never used the black leather armchair, which was reserved for Gabriel only. Between her thumb and her forefinger, far from her eyes, she held up a needle as she tried to thread it. Her eyes did not serve her as well as when she was younger, but she still tried to avoid glasses. At the moment when she was finally able to accomplish it by wetting the end of the threat with her saliva, the door to the room opened, and Jacob tried to sneak in. His movements suggested some shyness and unusual insecurity. Anybody but Theresa would easily consider them to be just a sign of his usual churlishness and manly timidity. But Theresa knew her sons and Jacob perhaps even better than the others.

When he entered, she lifted her eyes from her sewing and greeted him with a smile. Her face, however, became more serious as she immediately recognized that Jacob had not come just because of having nothing else to do, or because he wanted to cheer up his old mother. His heart seemed to be heavy. Heavy with something he could not solve. He had to get it out but did not know how.

Jacob stood next to the other window, looked at the backyard, and his fingers impatiently tapped on the window frame. He folded his hands behind his back. Then he walked twice around the table and then from the door to the wall and back. He paused at the basket where several apples were laid. He took one apple and broke it with his strong hands, but the apple was wormy, and he thus walked back to the window and threw the wormy half out and resumed the tapping on the window sill.

Theresa did not look up from her sewing, but her swift fingers stopped for a moment, and between two stitches, she remarked:

"It's stuffy, my boy. Don't you want a glass of milk?"

Jacob barely answered. He just mumbled something like that he was not thirsty and continued to pace the room. Stuffy, he thought. Stuffy. If only she knew what was stifling him. But how to confess it to her? And how to convince her to talk about it with Father? As a direct conversation with Father would be the most difficult, he hoped to delegate it to his mother. Mother will understand. She always understood everything. Rebecca will mourn, but her mourning will dry up quickly in the sand of her dull ordinariness. And the child that will be born? They will never meet, and in the end, it is Rebecca's child, not his. What could the father give to the child that was not conceived in love? No, Jacob was not worried about it. But Father, how will his father accept it? That question filled Jacob's heart with more fear than anything else.

He stopped at his father's armchair and unwittingly took a step back as if he felt his father's intent look underneath his thick and strict eyebrows. Theresa for a moment placed her hands with the sewing into her tender lap and caressed him with her affectionate glance:

"Doesn't my son Jacob want to tell me something?"

Jacob approached Theresa and gently took his mother's hand.

"I wanted to, Mother," he said with a downcast look. Then he stood up behind the backrest of Mother's chair so that she could not see his face, and he put his hands on her shoulders. She understood and did not turn around but touched twice with the warm palm of her veined hand his fingers, and with a soothing voice, she asked:

"And what is bothering my boy?"

He did not answer for a while. She just felt the trembling of his hot fingers on her shoulders and again touched his hand.

"So, tell me what is on your mind, just tell me."

"You have to help me, Mother," he exhaled.

"You know that I will help you. You know. But you have to tell me everything neatly in order."

He again remained silent. Then his words started to fall on Theresa's head like heavy drops that gradually change into a wild and destructive downpour. After the first words of Jacob's confession, Theresa froze, lifted her hand to her eyes, and wept a lot of bitter tears.

"O my God, my God, my God, why do you punish me?" she lamented. "Why did you send, in addition to all other trials on us, also this tragedy?"

"Don't speak like that, Mother, don't cry. I don't want you to be unhappy," Jacob bent down to her and hugged her head. "You understand me, you have to understand me, I cannot go on like this, it's terrible. I had a hard head, did not listen to your advice, and I got punished. But now, now I can be happy again, and you have to help me."

As if she did not hear him, she nodded her white head back and forth while whispering: "Poor Rebecca, poor child, poor Rebecca, poor child." And then, as if encountering a new horror, she shouted: "She is a *goyte*, a goyte! Poor Father, it will kill him."

She stood up fast as if she wanted to run to help somebody, but her legs buckled under her, and she dropped back into the chair. Jacob got on his knees and laid his head on her lap.

"You have to help me, Mother, you have to help me," he begged like a little boy, but Theresa continued to weep into her palms that covered her face. Through the fissures between the fingers of her veined hands, one could just hear always the same: "It will kill him, it will kill him."

But then, suddenly, like when she had started to sob, her tears stopped flowing. She dried her eyes with a handkerchief, straightened up in her chair, made Jacob stand up, and got back to her sewing. Only her voice sounded harder when she spoke again:

"What do you want? How should I help you?"

"I do not want to part company with my father. I want you to tell him. He will accept it better from you than from me."

They spoke calmly now, without excitement, as if it were just a routine part of life, something that had to be arranged. Theresa continued to sew, and Jacob leaned on his father's armchair. Even he never sat down on it.

"I cannot tell him about it," Theresa said harshly and resolutely. "It would kill him." After a while, she added in a softer voice: "Think it over, my boy, think it over well."

"I thought through everything and made my decision," Jacob replied, and he started to pace through the room with his hands behind his back again.

"Do you want to destroy Rebecca's and the child's lives? Consider it carefully, my boy, and do not take a rash step. Rebecca is not a bad wife."

"I already made my decision and cannot take it back," Jacob interrupted Theresa's praises of Rebecca.

"And where will you go?" she asked after a while.

"Anywhere. Just away. Away from here."

"Life is tough and meandering, my boy. You will get lost in it like in a forest," she warned.

"I am asking you for one thing only. Please tell it to Father in place of me," he interrupted her impatiently.

"No, no, my boy. I cannot do that. It would kill him," she repeated, for God knows how many times.

"You rather want me to waste my life next to Rebecca?" he angrily exploded. But Theresa just looked up from her sewing and fixed her gaze on Jacob so that he had to cast his eyes down. He regretted his words, and like in the act of reconciliation, he gently touched Mother's head that again started to shake with pity.

"O my boy, my boy," she whispered fearfully.

"Help me, Mother. I know that you will help me," he pressed again.

But Theresa just repeated: "You cannot want something like that from me, Jacob. Not that. I cannot do that."

He begged once more with his eyes, but the imploring look met only helpless sorrow in Theresa's face. He abruptly turned around and ran out through the door. She saw him as he rushed past the yard to the large entrance gate and disappeared behind it.

At that moment, she began to sob loudly. Painful and suffocating weeping shook her tender body, her sewing fell onto the floor, and the ball of thread ended up near the door. Near the door through which Jacob left a few minutes ago, near the cursed door through which they all left. So her favorite youngest one, her David, left years ago and never came back. So left Jacob just now. Will he return? Will he ever come back? My God, it seems that they were small children just yesterday. She laid them down into their beds and woke up often with a heart full of fear as she worried that they could wander away like little chicks. So many broken knees, so many patches on their pants! David once fell down from a tree, and Ruben was bitten in the face by a dog. And Jacob broke his leg on the frozen river. Oh God, oh God, everything seemed to happen just yesterday. She still saw everything before her eyes. But in fact, that all happened a long time ago. How many years passed since she heard them from the Torah during bar mitzvah for the first time, how many years passed since they left for work in the malting house with Gabriel, how many years passed since they brought home their brides. She was jealous of them, jealous of each one of them. That made sense, of course. When the wife comes, the son does not need his mother anymore. But they were not bad wives. She liked quiet Chana, who took away her favorite youngest, David. She liked the daughter of the brush-maker Tolnai, who took away Ruben. And she liked Hedwig, who twisted Moshe around her little finger. Even Rebecca was not a bad wife. In truth, she was not very smart and hardly laughed at all. But hadn't she and Gabriel begged and warned Jacob so many times before he married her? Oh God, how right they were. She would give everything she had to avoid what happened now. But Jacob was always obstinate, stubborn, and headstrong. Already when he was born, his big hard head almost cost her her life. And now, now he will kill Gabriel. He will not survive that, poor Gabriel.

The tears stopped flowing, and her weeping melted into a quiet pain. She stared into space out of the window, and every once in a while, her breasts shook with a whining sob. Once she woke up from a mournful dream, it was already almost dark.

She became frightened and quickly got up. She then smoothed back her hair using her hand and, with the small and shuffling steps of little old women, hurried to the door leading to the kitchen.

Theresa's haste was, however, not needed as Gabriel came back home that evening much later than usual. He was held up in the brewery as the owners did not like something about the last shipment of the malt. When he finished arguing with them without reaching any resolution, it was already too late to stop at home, and he went directly to the synagogue. Thus, he returned home after the evening services, but that did not distract him from his daily worries this time.

When he entered the room where the table was already set up, he took off his hat and put on the black velvet yarmulke instead. Then he grumpily asked about Jacob:

"Where is he? He was not at services. He is not here. Where is he wandering around?"

Theresa laid the dishes with the food on the table and tried to steer the conversation away from Gabriel's question.

"You got delayed at the brewery, no? How did it end up?"

"Don't even ask," he waved his hand, and the shadows on his face got even darker.

Theresa realized her mistake too late. He did not like it when she tried to talk to him about business. She thus quickly attempted to change the subject.

"Did Ruben pray with you?" she asked even though she knew the answer as Ruben was devout after his father and never missed any services. Gabriel just mumbled something into his beard and nodded in agreement.

"And he did not tell you anything?" she continued to ask.

"What was he supposed to tell me?"

"I do not know for sure yet, but I think they are expecting," she forced herself into a good mood though memories of the afternoon conversation with Jacob were still hanging heavily on her mind. "I think you will have one more grandchild."

"Really? You think so? How do you know that?" Gabriel came to life, and his appetite immediately improved.

"You know, we women always see that first."

"Hmm, and he did not boast about it."

She saw that his mood got better, and she suddenly decided. Should he learn about it, it would be better if he heard it from her. Jacob was right about it. She laid her hand softly on Gabriel's shoulder and quietly, carefully, as if she were carrying in her palms something even more fragile than glass, told him:

"Gabriel, there is other news, but it is not good news."

And as if she were guiding a child on the bridge over a chasm, Theresa started to unwind the thinnest silk out of the ball of Jacob's confession. Her words sounded like a quiet, conciliatory rain falling on the leaves of a one-hundred-year-old oak. But the tree would not accept the moisture, and its branches were collapsing under the weight. Gabriel abruptly pushed away the dish with its unfinished meal. He laboriously lifted his heavy body, took two steps to his armchair, and then slumped into it. He dug his fingers into the backrest and, without saying a word, stared stiffly in front of himself. His mouth, half-covered by his yellowish beard, was moving without uttering any sound.

"Calm down, for heaven's sake, Gabriel," Theresa started to cry loudly, and, frightened from seeing his face, she ran out to the kitchen for a glass of water. In her ears, it was resonating: "It will kill him, it will kill him!"

Only a gasping movement of his voiceless mouth and a mad rage of the bulging eyes in his pale face animated the petrified statue of the sitting old man. Then, as if all the strings suddenly broke, a mournful sigh escaped his breast, and Gabriel curled up in the armchair as a felled tree. That is how Theresa found him when she hurried back with a glass of water.

"Drink, it will help you," she said while fighting tears, and her shaky hand lifted the glass to his mouth.

But Gabriel suddenly straightened up, pushed Theresa's hand swiftly away so that the water splashed out, grabbed the cane that always stood leaning on the wall underneath the rack of pipes, and yelled:

"Where is he?"

A wave of raging anger made the blood wildly circulate in his veins.

"Where is he?" he yelled again and struck the ground with his cane. "I need to know where he is."

"Calm down, calm down, Gabriel, *menuche*, stay calm," she begged pleadingly while holding in her palms before her the half-spilled glass. "You will talk him out of it. I am sure he will listen."

"Talk him out of it? I will beat it out of his head," Gabriel raved. He jumped out of the armchair, and with a cane in his hand, he rushed to the door.

Theresa threw all of her petite body between Gabriel and the door.

"Not this way, Gabriel, not this way," she proclaimed in a strong voice and fastened her eyes on him. In her look, a pleading request merged with resoluteness. He wavered for a moment but once again shouted out:

"Let me go, do you hear me, let me go!"

She trembled, but kept her eyes on his face.

"Get out of my way!" he yelled, full of anger.

Her head started to rock, but her tender voice remained as firm as before:

"Not this way, Gabriel. Rebuke him after you calm down. Not now. Sleep on it and rethink it again. I hope Jacob can still change his mind."

But Gabriel became almost insane.

"I do not have to think anything through. I will beat him like a dog. Like a dog! I will kill him! He is not my son anymore. Do not protect him! Get out of my way, go away, and let me go!"

She stretched her trembling hands towards him, still holding the half-empty glass of water, and cried into his face:

"In that case, kill me instead!"

His eyes became bloodshot, and while half-mad, he raised his hand with the cane as if he intended to hit her.

Theresa's lips just whispered: *"Sma 'Jisroel."* Then she dropped the glass, and her body slid slowly and lifelessly down the door to the ground. Then she dissolved into helpless tears.

Gabriel again froze. His raised hand fell heavily down, and his palm dropped the cane. He staggered towards the window but again slumped like a heavy boulder into the black armchair. Then he pressed his palms to his eyes, and his anger broke into decrepit weeping.

So they sobbed till the night looked on with its darkened eye through the window into the room. Then they both got up and slowly dragged themselves to bed.

Chapter 12

Seeking Advice

They did not sleep that night. Theresa laid motionlessly on her back while her eyes roved about the ceiling. She heard Gabriel tossing and turning from side to side next to her, but she was afraid to break the silence of the night and tried to hide that she was not asleep. She guessed that any word she would say would only add fuel to the flames in his heart.

And Gabriel's heart was burning with an uncontrollable fire. Flames of anger were blazing in him, and dark malice smoldered inside. He cursed Jacob, was tortured by the thought that he himself had caused it, and that he himself had allowed his son to leave the pathways of the fear of God. He called punishment down on Jacob's head, but then he immediately blamed himself for his own short temper, and his helpless ravings suffocated him. As he fell into a perplexed resignation, he asked himself what Philip would do. As under the shovels of good soil, sparks of anger were becoming extinguished once he thought about his friend. Why was everything much easier for Philip? So many times he tried to contemplate why Philip never lost his composure, why he never rushed things, and why he never raised a fist to make a threat. He again saw in front of himself the Rosh Hakol and the butcher how they stood against each other like the bulls, and he again heard Philip's short sentence that turned the hotheads down. What would Philip do if he were in his place now? Would he find another strong word? Would he drive Jacob out of the house how he himself would do right now, how he had to do right now? Or would he still believe that meekness and kindness were better than the fist and the cane? Talk to him, talk to him, he heard Theresa's voice. But everything revolted inside of him again. What could talking solve at this moment? What else was left besides a whip with which he would crack Jacob out of the door? But he still asked, again and again, what Philip would do?

Those worries consumed him till sunrise. When at seven o'clock Philip knocked on the window, Gabriel was already waiting. They walked together like in the old days. The baker again reported with sadness in his voice that Yitzhak did not write, and Philip's dog was swaying behind his master.

And like the other days, after the prayers, they said goodbye to each other before returning home and back to their work. Only the thick eyebrows above Gabriel's eyes seemed to become even thicker and the wrinkles on his face even deeper, but his words became sparser.

Jacob was not at the services as he found the work outside the house, and Gabriel did not look for him. He ate lunch without saying a word but bit the ends of his beard, yellowish from smoking. But once he finished the meal, he could not control himself anymore and abruptly left without any explanations.

This time, he himself picked up Philip without waiting for their usual hour. He could not wait. He needed an answer to the question of what Philip would do if he was in his position. Philip was the only person whom he trusted and whose advice he was willing to seek.

"What happened?" Philip greeted him with surprise as he looked up while kneading a lump of putty. In the corner, leaning on the wall, stood a broken window. And on the table was a photo of a young man in a military uniform, waiting to be framed. The man in the picture was the son of a rich Beluša widow. Like David Menasse, he had not returned from the war, but his mother never lost hope that he would one day come back. Those were the jobs lined up for Philip's afternoon. But Gabriel just said:

"Leave it here and come with me to the Small Grove."

As Gabriel's face looked pretty solemn, Philip wiped his hands, untied the protective apron that he wore above his clothes while at work, and left with Gabriel for a walk at this unusual hour.

Daniel sat in front of the house and played with the dog. He turned him over onto his back, scratched him on the belly, and laughed at the rapid movements of his short rear legs that were pawing into the air to the rhythm of the boy's touches. When they saw both old men exiting the building, they joyfully jumped up from the ground and rushed to them.

"May I come with you?" Daniel pleaded.

"You may, but you have to be quiet," said Grandpa Philip. "And let Mom know so that she does not look for you."

Daniel jumped up, opened the door to the store, and while the bell attached to the door frame announced his entry, he called to Chana:

"Mom, I am going with Grandpa."

Then he pulled Dak's long silk ear as Dak jumped around him while wagging his tail, and Daniel started to run. The dog rushed behind him with his tongue hanging out.

It was an unwritten rule that Philip and Gabriel did not begin to talk until they reached Creekside Street as there were almost no people there. But before they got there, they simply silently walked next to each other, Philip with his hands behind his hunched back and Gabriel holding the pipe at his mouth as even during those strolls, he never stopped smoking. From time to time, on the street where the baker Spitzer lived or when they crossed the town square, one of them would utter something important while not yet expecting an answer. Today, however, all the rules were broken, and Philip guessed there had to be something quite serious behind Gabriel's decision to come to Philip instead of waiting for his knock on the window. Something had happened to Gabriel. He saw it on his face when he came, and later, he also noticed that Gabriel did not light his pipe and just ground it between the teeth.

He shuffled, but his short steps were fast so that he could keep up with Gabriel's brisk strides. He, however, contemplated in vain what his friend was struggling with. He only came up with two things that, according to his mind, could bother

Gabriel. Perhaps it is the sale of the Torahs. Aaron Timfeld had convinced others to invite Braun from Břeclav. He argued that in the end, nothing would happen if they just asked him to look at them and to tell them the price. Braun was supposed to arrive the day after tomorrow, and perhaps Gabriel wanted to discuss something about that case. The second possibility that crossed his mind scared Philip more. Was it possible that the misery affecting everybody was now forcing Gabriel to ask for a loan? He knew that Gabriel had had some difficulties with the brewery recently and owed some money to the farmers for the barley. But was it possible that his situation had become so unbearable that he did not know what else to do? And what will he tell him if he asks him? Can he say to him that he himself is hanging onto his last thread?

When they crossed the town square and were passing the church, he could not hold it in anymore and asked Gabriel directly:

"What is worrying you?"

Gabriel removed the pipe from his mouth as if he wanted to answer. But suddenly, it was too difficult for him to speak and form sentences from the words as the words seemed to be stuck in his mouth, and he did not know how to begin. He just sighed and continued to walk.

However, once they were halfway through Creekside Street and Philip repeated his question, Gabriel's tongue loosened. Angry charges against Jacob and his sin fell out from Gabriel's chest like an avalanche of stones. They were interrupted by sobbing and cursing, by repressed moans and the helpless clasping of hands, but also by Philip's soothing.

"Is having children worthy?" Gabriel asked at the end with a broken voice and in tears. "What ingratitude. That is how children pay you back for your kindness."

"Don't blaspheme," Philip told him.

"I will throw him out. He is not my son anymore. He is dead to me. I will sit *shiva* for him," abruptly came from Gabriel's chest.

"Gabriel," Philip attempted to soothe him, "Gabriel!"

"What else can I do?" he asked helplessly. "What should I do?"

Philip did not answer. He just tapped his friend on the shoulder as they continued their stroll through the tree-lined road around the creek. On its surface, dried-up leaves were floating, prematurely turned yellow from the blazing heat of the sun. Daniel was running back and forth around the old men, playing tag with the dog, and collecting cockchafers that fell from the trees while pretending that he was not paying attention to his grandfathers' conversation.

After a while, Philip asked:

"And what does Theresa say?"

"What does she say? Talk to him, she says, talk to him," he exploded and angrily waved his hand into the air.

"Mothers tend to be usually right, Gabriel," remarked Philip. "Mothers are always right."

"I cannot. I would kill him. I would kill him like a dog."

"Gabriel," Philip was soothing him again.

"I cannot. I am telling you, I cannot," Gabriel repeated.

They still walked along the creek. Once they reached the end of the tree-lined road where they usually made a turn to the Small Grove, Philip said:

"Do you want me to talk to Jacob?"

Gabriel helplessly spread out his hands, shrugged his broad shoulders that had lost their fighting spirit a while ago, and powerlessly answered:

"If you want to, talk to him."

They did not go to the Small Grove. Instead, they turned around at the end of the tree-lined street and returned back to the road by the creek. In Gabriel's heart, a spark of new hope seemed to be born. He felt relieved but was afraid to show it. Even for Philip, it was a weight off his mind once he realized that Gabriel's worries were about something other than what he had feared. But the secret of Gabriel's agony was too grave, and the task Philip had taken upon himself was too hard that they could not utter even a single word about anything else. They thus walked next to each other, and only their shuffling steps in the fallen leaves interrupted the silence.

Daniel stopped jumping around the old men and trailed behind them with his hands in his pockets, and, lost in thought, he looked to the ground. Every once in a while, he kicked the stones or stood up to rush towards Dak, who was tired from the wild romping with the boy, and dragged his long body on his short curved legs behind his master while maintaining a more than respectful distance.

So they went and remained silent. He will talk to Jacob, thought Gabriel. Philip will talk to Jacob. Hopefully. Hopefully, he will be able to do that. Philip is the only one who can do that. Gabriel himself would crack him out of the house with the whip. Maybe he would even kill him. Even if Theresa wept as much as she was able, she could not move Jacob's unrepentant heart. Only Philip can perhaps find the most appropriate words. Philip always finds the right words. Of course, it will be one more defeat for Gabriel, but why should he resist defeat when it saves his son. Only Philip can find the right words, Gabriel was convincing himself.

But Philip was also deliberating. Oh God, what a task he had assigned to himself. What will he tell Jacob? What will he tell him? That he will break his father's heart? That Theresa will worry to death for him? That his child will grow without a home? Will it be helpful? Oh God, we all were also once young. Can you convince a runaway stallion to stop so that he would not trample his master to death? What will he tell him? What should he tell him? O God, O God, how hard it is!

Daniel, who trailed behind the old men, was also trying to sort out everything in his head. So Grandpa already knows. And it did not have to come from silly David. Jacob himself made a confession. And did it not demonstrate that Uncle Jacob was not a bad man?

Perhaps he was better than Daniel himself. Whenever he did anything wrong, he never confessed to it if nobody else knew about it. No, David was not right. Uncle Jacob was not bad. And Grandfather was also not telling the whole truth.

Was it Jacob's fault that he did not like Aunt Rebecca? Daniel also does not like her. She never smiles like Mom, she never plays with him like Grandpa Philip, she never offers him an apple like Grandma Theresa, and she hardly talks. And she is also not pretty.

How could Uncle Jacob like her? But he married her. And they are expecting a baby. And that seemed to be quite terrible to Daniel. For that, Uncle Jacob deserved punishment. For that, God will for sure punish him. Or would punish him if he were just like Grandfather Gabriel says. But he already knows that he is not right. And even if he were right, God and not Grandfather would have to punish Jacob. And if Grandfather really believed that God was just, why was he getting so angry? But if God does not punish Uncle Jacob even though he is just, then perhaps what Uncle Jacob did was not as appalling.

Daniel was again at the end of his tether. He tried in vain to untangle the fibers of the tangled ball of his thoughts. Oh God, how is everything so tangled, he thought. I wonder how God and Grandpa Philip will untangle it.

So they walked back through the tree-lined street along the creek without saying a word, but they all thought about the same thing. The sun hid behind the clouds and the dry leaves above their heads rustled in a light breeze, coming from the fields in the west.

Once they reached the end of the tree-lined road, Philip suddenly stopped and carefully inspected the creek's surface. There was a cockchafer tossing around in the center of the stream after he fell from the tree. He was lying on his wing cases while floating down on them like on a dinghy, and his legs, pointing up to the sky, were just helplessly waving in the air. Philip laid down on the ground next to the bank and bent half of his body over the water so that he could grab the drowning cockchafer.

"*Sma 'Jisroel*, what are you doing?" marveled Gabriel.

"This one can still be saved," Philip called from the ground. Then he got up on his knees while holding the cockchafer in his palm and, using the other hand, tried to straighten out his tousled wing cases. He then dried up the cockchafer with his handkerchief, and once Gabriel helped him to stand up on his feet, he said:

"Do you see? This one could still be saved." And then he handed the cockchafer to Gabriel while adding:

"You are taller. Here he is. Put him back on the tree."

Gabriel looked for a while at Philip's palm and just shook his head. Then he took the cockchafer with two fingers, extended himself as much as possible, and placed him on a forked branch above the road but far from the creek.

Then they continued further, but kept silent like before. But the spark of hope in Gabriel's heart burst into a flame. "This one can be still saved," he heard, again and again, Philip's words. But he thought about Jacob.

Chapter 13

Remorse

"I have already told you, gentlemen, this is the right price, and that is how much I could give you. No more and no less."

Antique dealer Braun who arrived on that day from Břeclav to inspect the treasures the kehilla was reluctantly considering selling, was a short and plump guy with golden nose-glasses and a golden chain on his belly. Besides an old watch, he also carried in his vest pocket a magnifying glass, and his tiny fat fingers with a richly decorated signet ring kept playing with it at the moment. Underneath his sleeves were revealed rubber cuffs fastened together with a garnet button. Underneath the left cuff peeked out the tip of a handkerchief that he took out from time to time and wiped his sweaty bald head after raising his black but somewhat faded bowler hat.

"No more and no less," he repeated. Then he once more raised the magnifying glass to his eye to look at the hallmark on the silver bells of one of the Torahs that were spread out in front of him on the long table in the back section of the synagogue.

"It is not as old as I had initially thought," he expertly remarked as if he tried to provide some explanation. Then he turned directly to Aaron Timfeld, who stood in the center of the group: "So what do you think, Mr. Rosh Hakol, will we close the deal?" Then he glanced from underneath his golden nose-glasses at the others before he asked: "And what do you think, gentlemen?"

They sat and stood in small groups around the table. On the table were spread out Torah scrolls dressed up in velvet covers with golden embroidery, tiny silver bells, cups, candlesticks, menorahs, Mizrachs, chains, and yad pointers with a small hand at the end that were used during the reading from the

Torah. Their eyes wandered over those treasures, gathered by generations of their fathers, grandfathers, and great grandfathers. They did not talk and appeared despondent as if they had just heard a disagreeable verdict. In their minds, pity was mixed with shame, with the pity caused by the departure from an inherited treasure, and the shame caused by the poverty that forced them to take this humiliating step. They were also mystified or almost insulted by the price offered by Ignatius Braun, as it was much lower than what they had expected.

Now, when he posed a direct question to them, they looked at each other with timidity and shyness, coughed slightly, moved along, pushed the chairs, and waited to see who would be willing to break the awkward silence first. Aaron Timfeld walked to his armchair with a high backrest, sat down, and started to talk.

"You have heard the offer," he said, and his gaze roamed from one to the other without making any direct eye contact. "You have heard. Now please make your comments."

But one could only hear slight coughing and the helpless shuffling of the chairs, but nobody was brave enough to initiate the conversation. Finally, the traveling salesman Kantůrek got up from the very end of the long table and raised his hand. "If the gentlemen allow, I would have a suggestion," his voice squeaked as if it were spread with goose dripping. His eyes-without-eyelashes blinked, and he pressed the fingertips on both hands against each other. "If the gentlemen were not against it and if Mr. Braun here kindly agreed with it, Mr. Braun might kindly go out for a few moments so that they could discuss his kind offer among themselves. But only if the gentlemen here agreed with it."

This time, everybody agreed with Kantůrek, and Braun was willing to give them an opportunity to discuss in privacy and in his absence the offer he gave them. He simply turned around in the doorway and, while playing with the magnifying glass, said:

"I am just asking you, gentlemen, not to take too much time. I would like to get back home before dark."

So they were on their own amongst themselves and began to deliberate. Lebenhart was the first to start:

"No. No way. Definitely not. Such a price! That is unheard of!" he uttered angrily and with each additional "no" was becoming all riled up.

"I also think no," remarked Beinhacker, who was sitting at the opposite end of the table from Lebenhart, and his voice was calmer than usual. "We cannot accept something like that."

"So, give us some other suggestions," Timfeld quickly retorted.

Silence fell again till Philip Taub said:

"Braun is an honest man. When he says that that is the price, nobody except us will value it more. Nobody would pay us more than that."

"What kind of honesty is it," countered the butcher who was getting back into his form. "Business is business, and for Braun, this is nothing more than making a purchase at a price that he can make a good *revoch*."

"An honest man! And such a price! That is unheard of," seconded Lebenhart.

"We definitely have to negotiate," remarked Tolnai.

"That goes without saying," agreed Kahan.

"At least we can try," added the wagoner. "We cannot lose anything by trying."

So far, Gabriel Menasse sat quietly between Philip Taub and Abeš Tolnai and stared into space. But now he roused from his daydreaming and muttered under his breath:

"Do we have to make a final decision on it right now? I believe we came here only to learn what the price of all of it is."

"Yes," Aaron Timfeld calmly answered. "But we know that we are flat broke, and should we accept Braun's offer, it would help us for a while. Perhaps till better times come."

Gabriel just mumbled something and withdrew back into the shell of his own mind. He was preoccupied with other worries.

"Definitely, we must also request another offer," Klein got

back to the topic that was interrupted by Gabriel Menasse.

"Of course. That's right. Without question," sounded from all the sides. Only Philip repeated that Ignatius Braun was an honest man and that nobody would give them more than Braun's offer. But the majority was clearly against him. And the traveling salesman Kantůrek got up again at the end of the table and offered with his squeaky voice that he could also talk to another antique dealer he knew, to Weiss from Trnava. If the gentlemen here agreed, he could also request an offer from him.

"We are dead broke," Timfeld forcibly stressed again as he already made his own decision. "We have an opportunity here. Let's not lose it by raising unnecessary obstacles. I am telling you again that we are broke. We are flat broke. Let's try to get more money from Braun. I agree with that. But let's not postpone it any longer."

It sounded so pleading from the cautious mouth of Timfeld that everybody understood the warning. They stopped talking about the postponement of the deal and began to deliberate about the price they should put up against Braun's offer and from which they could take a little off in order to reach a sum agreeable to Braun. They were weighing the price on delicate scales so that it would not be too high to discourage Braun from any negotiation, but also not too low so that Braun would accept it too easily, to their regret. Finally, they decided on the value.

Then, however, Philip Taub got up from his seat. He did not participate in the negotiations about the price, but his trembling voice with which he turned to Timfeld immediately quietened their tongues, which were excited from the bargaining.

"We forgot about one thing," he said, and his eyes looked at them pleadingly. "We will have holidays soon, my friends, high holidays." He grabbed the handkerchief, cleared up his nose, and continued: "We were always carrying all the Torahs in all their glamor. Does it have to be different this year? Could we not wait with the sale until after the holidays?"

He finished his speech and sat down. Everybody got silent, and they again experienced those feelings of pity and shame. Until the moment when Timfeld coughed slightly, winked several times, and said the final word:

"Of course. I have not forgotten about it. We will tell Braun only the price we have negotiated today, but will make the sale after the holidays."

They muttered their agreement, and Kantůrek went for the antiquarian who was waiting behind the door. When he entered, Timfeld shared with him the decision of the kehilla.

"Sounds good, gentlemen, sounds good," Braun smiled. "If you want to bargain, we will bargain. But you should have thought it through before asking me to come," he added annoyed, "and you could have called for me after the holidays."

Timfeld promised to write him right after the holidays. Braun looked at his watch and left as he wanted to be at home before dark.

Once they were on their own again, they took all the Torahs into their hands. They carried them through the aisle between the pews to the other end of the synagogue, into the cabinet behind the altar. Once the last one was there, they closed the red plush curtain that was embroidered with the golden Lion of Judah holding Tablets of the Law and with an inscription in Hebrew:

"From the rising of the sun to its going down
the Lord's name is to be praised."

Chapter 14

Martin

Kohút's pub was throbbing with life once again. Kohút, a hefty fellow with a belly like a barrel covered with an apron, and his dark-haired daughter Marka were serving a lot of drams on the table. People were for sure short on money, but today, Nasťa Okáník delivered a son, and it was the first son of Martin Pálkovič, and they thus had to celebrate. What a great woman Nasťa was. Martin was proud of her. Just yesterday, she worked in the beet field, but her hour came this past night. Grandma Okáník helped, and by the morning, a boy was born. What else could it be than a boy? Such a cute baby boy, and his eyes are blue like his father's. Life is tough but at the same time beautiful, thought Martin, and he started to sing. Others joined him.

They thus sat around the rough table without a tablecloth. The happy father was joined by the old Okáník, the wild Klvaňa, and the sickly Palo Markovič. The gangling Tomík and always serious and quiet Gabaňa also came to drink a toast to Martin's son. The blasphemer Pišta Gavora limped in there as well, and even Ferenčák, whose job was to stand in front of the pub to maintain order, could not resist and entered to wet his beard with the brandy.

"O, I am drinking, I am drinking,
I drank away all I had..."

The song, coming out of their hoarse throats, was filling the darkened room, thick with smoke. Except for a kerosene lamp hanging on the wall, the only light objects were Kohút's apron and Marka's round calves.

They stopped singing, and on the table, Marka laid in front of them another round of drams. Once they wet their whistles with the booze, Gabaňa was the first to loosen his tongue:

"So, how will you call him, Martin?"

"How should they call him? Martin, of course, after his dad," instead of the father, Grandfather Okáník answered the question.

"Yes, that sounds good. Call him Martin," others agreed.

"A poor thing," remarked Gavora.

"A poor thing? Why a poor thing?" wondered Martin.

"And you think he will be grateful to you that you brought him into this lousy world?" Pišta ground out and spat into the corner.

"Why lousy, I like it as it is. And especially today, I really like it," smiled Martin and raised the empty glass to Marka so that she could fill it up again. When she approached the table, Klvaňa slapped her round bottom so that she shouted.

"Of course. Everybody knows that the world is nice and round like you, Marka," he grinned and pulled her to himself. But Kohút's apron showed up at the bar, and he immediately let her go.

"So it is nice, well, nice," Pišta Gavora did not abandon the train of thought he started. "And that in winter, there will not be enough holes on your belt once you try to tighten it up, that is also nice. And that there is no rye and no vine, and the beet is not good enough to dig it out, that is also nice. And that you will have to slaughter your last cow, that is also nice. There is so much beauty in the world." He knocked his glass back for a second and landed the empty cup loudly on the table.

"That's how it is," Okáník grew sad, and his droopy walrus beard hung down from his unhappy mouth. "That's how it is. God abandoned us. We will perish. We all will perish."

"Oh well, why are you complaining, grandpa," Palo Markovič soothed him. "We have not died yet. Rather be happy that you got a grandson."

But the old man's head was just nodding.

"God has not abandoned us," Tomík explained. "We have abandoned the God. But he is merciful and will help us," he added after a while and turned his eyes above to the sooty ceiling around which clouds of smoke billowed.

"Go away with your God," Gavora said and spat again. "He did help you, didn't He?"

It was hanging over their hearts like a heavy fog that prevented any sunlight from coming in. Every day, every step, every look at the dry field, and every dig with a hoe led, again and again, to hundreds of variations of the same conversation. There was always somebody here who blasphemed like Gavora, always somebody pious like Tomík, always somebody desperate like Okáník, and always somebody with a soothing voice similar to the soothing earnestness of Palo Markovič.

Mothers taught them the Hail Mary and Our Father and dressed them up in clean shirts before taking them to church for a mass. Like annual rings in the tree trunk, the faith traditions grew in them with years. They turned to God in their worries as they believed in one truth, in one grace, and in one justice. But often, too often, difficulties in their lives led them to the bank of doubts, and despair bored through their faith like a woodworm. Like in the forest where one tree is affected deeper than the others, there were differences among them as well. Some of them, like Tomík, had a hard core, and the worms' mandibles did not destroy them. But the pulp of others like Pišta Gavora was already gnawed through and through, and the rotting inside often ignited on its own. It was thus hanging over them each step of the way. They asked all the time but never received any answer. Just believe, believe, believe, preached the priest in the church. But to believe in God who is sending down the drought and blight into their vineyards. Why, why?

"God knows what He is doing," Tomík said, but before Pišta could again explode with anger, Gabaňa started to talk.

"Oh well, stop it. You will not come up with anything new anyway."

And Palo Markovič rushed to his aid.

"That's right. Let's stop it for today. Let's forget about

everything, and let's drink to Martin's son." He raised the glass that stood in front of him on the table and emptied it in one go. And Marka was back again with a bottle of brandy and refilled their cups all over again.

"Leave that flask here," Klvaňa grinned, grabbed the bottle, and hugged Marka again around her hips. "Better give me a kiss," he said and cuddled up to her. She broke away from him with a smile, and Klvaňa just waved a hand behind her.

"You silly goose," he vented, "so much shouting for one little kiss. A nice woman under the blanket is all a man needs. What do you think, Martin?" He looked at Martin, and his eyes were bleary and glassy from the booze, but he still drained another dram. Then his fist pounded on the table so forcefully that the cups rang, and his rough voice sounded:

"Chaps are drinking
in a stone pub,
everybody is thinking
they are outlaws just."

Others joined in. Only Tomík grasped the empty glass with the bony fingers of both of his hands and looked up somewhere at the sooty ceiling.

It was getting late, and Ferenčák got up. It was his time. He had to walk around the streets of the town, blow his horn at each corner, and sing softly:

"Twelve o'clock struck,
all souls praise the Lord..."

Chapter 15

Karolek

Jacob was coming back to work after finishing his lunch. He was lost in thought, and his eyes focused on the packed down ground of the courtyard, which he measured with long and firm-looking strides. Then suddenly, the dry cracking of broken glass reverberated around, and its shattered pieces rained down from the window above him.

"O my God, what a clumsy clod am I," Theresa's lamentation sounded behind the window. "My God, my God, I am really getting old."

Jacob approached the wall, looked inside, and once he saw that the chips did not injure his mother, he smiled at her frightened face.

"Mother, what happened?"

"I just wanted to set Father's cane straight," she tried to explain, "but once I turned around, you can see what happened. My God, I am a clumsy old clod," she continued to lament. "And Father will get mad," she added, and suddenly she looked up at him and begged: "Jacob, could you bring it to Philip? I am sure he would glaze it right away. You could wait until it is done. I would send Barbara there, but you know that she is not very reliable. Go, my boy, go and do it for your old clumsy mother. And please make sure that you bring it back before Father returns. Ask Philip to be quick with it." And she again pleaded with her eyes: "Will you go?"

Jacob was amused by her apprehensive worries of a fearful chicken. He did not realize how well Theresa played her role. He just smiled at Mother's wailing about the broken window that rather resembled the mourning for the destruction of the Temple in Jerusalem. He could not resist teasing her.

"Do you remember how I was beaten when I broke the window?" he asked with mock seriousness.

"Jacob," she again asked timidly, and he started to unhinge the window.

"So we are fine now," he smiled while trying to imitate the benevolence with which she used to forgive his boyish trespasses when he was a child. "But I am telling you, make sure it does not happen again."

Then he cleaned the frame from the remaining pieces of glass, put it on his shoulder, and got through the gate in front of the house.

He had to think about Mother. How much he loved her. How much he liked her white and always neatly combed hair, those quiet, deep, always a little scared but at the same time comforting eyes, those hands, bluish from a network of veins, waterlogged from washing, pricked all over from sewing, but always ready to help. How much would he like to sometimes lift her up like a feather and spin her around like a child. But Jacob and Theresa were never ones to show too much tenderness. Once in a while, they caressed each other with their eyes. Once in a while, they shared a timid touch, and they gave one yearly hug during the *Shana Tovah* greeting in front of the synagogue, and that was all.

He crossed the empty town square with the window on his shoulder, passed Creekside Street, and entered the small road where Philip's house stood. My mother, my mom, he was thinking. There was always a little girl inside of her. Perhaps because of that, she was the only person who could always bring peace back into his heart. She was able to do that even now when his soul was quite far from being calm. But is there not inside of every woman at least a bit of a little girl? In Helen, who continues to dress like a princess and who plays with the shadows from her fingers on the wall? In Rebecca? No, nothing from a little girl was left in Rebecca. Nothing from a little girl enjoying a game. That was it. That was the root of everything. Green pastures ended here, and the desert was taking a hold, the eternal and gray desert from which he must escape.

The weight that was briefly lifted by the thoughts about Mother returned to his feet when he entered Philip's store. The bell on the door announced his arrival. Chana rushed there from the kitchen while wiping her wet hands in an apron, and she ushered him inside.

"Father is in the workshop," she said when she noticed a shattered window on Jacob's shoulder. She raised the folding board that served as a bridge between the two counters and took Jacob into a small room behind the store.

"You are bringing some work for me?" Philip greeted him with a smile.

He stood next to a large table that filled the entire half of the workshop and on which the glazier's tools were spread out. Nails, cutters, glazier's diamond, old razor blades, wooden as well as metal rulers, hammers, pliers, and bottles with varnish were lying adjacent to small pieces of glass and mirrors and parts of frame ledges. In the center of the desk, there was a brown wrapping paper with a large clod of putty that he was kneading using both hands.

In the other half of the dark workshop into which the light only got through the glass door to the store and from where a kerosene lamp that was suspended from the blackened ceiling had to burn all the time stood an old worn-out shelf full of books and on the wall above it hung the picture of Philip's deceased wife. In the corner, there was a rocking chair, but its netting was ragged. Here Philip sat in stolen moments, rocking in the chair and quietly singing sentences from the sacred books. But only in the winter or when it rained. When the weather was nice, he read daily for a few moments outside in the backyard. On those days, he carried out a wicker armchair with a discolored pillow on the backrest and placed it underneath the apricot tree.

He was now standing at the table, covered with a greasy blue apron, and was holding putty in his hands. As he greeted Jacob, he was trying to sort out how to start the conversation.

He promised Gabriel that he would talk to Jacob, and without a doubt, he was sent here by Theresa. She had woven it really well. But the task was on his shoulders now. What will he tell Jacob? He thought about it for the entire day yesterday but had not come up with anything. Even now, he still did not know. Should he confess that he is well aware of the situation with Helen, and should he carefully try to talk him out of it? Should he speak through the parables of the holy books so that Jacob would understand? His hands kneading the brown putty started to move faster as if they were trying to knead the answer out of the clay.

Jacob shifted from one foot to the other. He put the window on the floor and propped it against the edge of the table. He then shyly answered Philip's greetings:

"We broke this one. Could you please fix it right away?"

Philip looked aside at the broken window but did not stop working.

"I will fix it," he said, "of course I will. Just don't try to rush me. I will begin as soon as I prepare the putty."

"May I wait for it?" Jacob asked.

"You may," Philip quickly replied, and he showed him the rocking chair. "You can sit down here with me for a moment. I wanted to talk to you anyway."

To talk, to talk, he thought, but how? Will the words he was trying in vain to find suddenly come out of his mouth? He turned the clod and kneaded it from the other side.

"With me? And about what?" Jacob asked surprised. He sat down into the chair, and its netting cracked under his weight.

"You'll see," Philip said, and he started to roll the softened putty. The words, my God, the words, he prayed quietly. "Just so," he said after a while, and then as if he suddenly made a decision, he turned to Jacob with both an affectionate and at the same time reproachful look:

"Why don't we see you in the services more often?"

Oh no, in addition to everything else, he starts with this, Jacob thought to himself. Father most likely incited him to do that, and though his head was exploding with his own worries, he will have to listen to a sermon about his godlessness. Mother really could not pick up a better day to break that dumb window, and he stupidly had to run with it here right away. And now he stands before that good-natured old man who taught him to make kites when he was a little boy. He wipes his hands in his apron and keeps an eye on him while waiting to see if he will tell him why he does not go to shul more often. So let him know it.

"And what should I search there for?" he answered angrily. But Philip's eyes did not lose their kindness. He just told him slowly and without any fury:

"For God, Jacob. For God and for peace."

Then he turned towards the table, measured the opening in the window frame, took a glass sheet leaning on the wall in the corner, laid a metal ruler on top of it, and put a diamond to the glass. The glass hissed under the hard tip and creaked dryly when he broke it around the cut.

Is he taking an appropriate route? he asked himself at that moment. Will it lead somewhere with Jacob?

He laid the frame on the table, placed the cut-out glass into the opening, and started to attach it using small tacks that he nailed into the wood where he removed the remaining old putty. Jacob, meanwhile, was listening to the squeaky sound of the hammer as it touched the glass edge while sitting motionlessly in the rocking chair and clasping its backrest tightly.

What was the purpose of this talk about God? Indeed, he could always speak about it more freely with Philip than with his own father. But hadn't he finished with all those questions a while ago? His head was really not ready for those discussions now. How will it help him? But he could not resist answering:

"I am telling you I have been going to shul for a long time, and I have not found Him there."

Philip looked up for a moment from his work:

"We have to search for God all the time. And we are not

allowed to stop searching." He grabbed a piece of putty, rolled it into a narrow roll, and started to lay it around the edges of the frame on the border between the wood and the glass.

"To search," Jacob exploded suddenly, "to search. To search for somebody who may not even exist."

He paused. He did not want to hurt the old man and realized too late how hard his words had likely affected him. Philip's old hand that was holding the knife he used for cutting off the excess putty and smoothing out the brown trim trembled a little and stopped working for a moment. But only for a moment. Philip did not even look up from his table while deciding how to proceed.

"I will tell you something, Jacob," he said and tried to hide the trembling in his voice. "Something I have never said to anybody. Not even to your father. He would not understand. But you might understand. I will tell it to you only because, or it does not matter why, but I will share it with you. You are saying that God perhaps does not exist. Perhaps He doesn't, Jacob. Perhaps He really does not exist. We do not know. We can only believe. But we will never know for sure."

That surprised Jacob. Only if he had perhaps heard those words from his father would he have been more surprised than when he heard them from Philip's mouth.

"But in that case, why pray to somebody who may not even exist?"

"Be patient, Jacob. Let me finish my point," continued Philip. He was done with his work, but he remained bent over the glazed window and turned with his back towards Jacob as he did not want to look into his eyes. "We will never know. Nobody will ever know. We are pitiful, Jacob. Oh God, how pitiful we are. We all, we all are pitiful because we will never know. We are like children in the darkness. Like children in a thick forest. And because of that, perhaps only because of that, we have to be kind. We have to be kind to each other. We have to hold our hands in the darkness to at least not lose each other. It is said that we should love each other, Jacob. We truly should. But most importantly, we have to feel pity for others, for those who are as pitiful as us, or perhaps even more than us."

He turned towards Jacob now. He stood there, small and more hunched than usual, and wiped the putty off from his hands and into the apron around his waist. He glanced for a moment at the picture above the shelf with books and continued wistfully:

"Love, Jacob, sometimes vanishes. Not always. But often it does. Yet pity, pity has to stay in us. We have to keep it in mind every step. Only in that way will we not hurt anybody. Whoever has enough pity will rather hurt himself. Whoever has pity in his heart carries life much easier. Whoever does not have it will perish."

He paused and then added with a smile:

"But I am preaching here, and you are in a rush, aren't you? You know, I have no son, and that is why I am telling all of this to you, as if you were my son."

It did not appear to Jacob to ask why Philip had told him all of that. He sat in the corner of Philip's workshop and was grateful for the twilight that allowed him to hide his stare. Philip's words fell like soft rain on his head. But at the same time, they were engraved into his conscience like a sharp tip of the diamond with which the old man a while ago defeated the hardness of the glass.

He finished some time ago, but Jacob remained sitting there motionlessly with his eyes downcast. Then he got up and, without saying a word, put the glazed window on his shoulder and got ready to leave.

But then suddenly, one could hear a desperate shriek arising from the street, so loud that it reached through the store to Philip's workshop. It did not resemble a human voice, but there was still no doubt that it came out of a human throat. They ran in front of the house and saw the fool Karolek standing in the middle of the road. Tears poured down the giant's round face. He was in tatters and was dragging Ivanko's dog behind him on a strong rope. Gipsy attempted to resist while howling ruefully.

"Bad, bad," Karolek cried madly, and only with difficulty would one recognize words in his desperate and ferocious shrieks. "Bad, ba-a-ad," he whimpered mournfully.

People ran out of all the houses around the road, covered with parched mud. Women with wet aprons as they left the scrubbing boards, men as they abandoned their work, scared children interrupted from their play, they all with fright on their faces, asked what happened. But the fool always only uttered the same word.

They talked to him, showered him with questions, but he just repeated the same sounds, and from his shrieks, they could understand no more than from Gipsy's prolonged howling. But Philip stood in front of him and lifted his hands up. Karolek stopped, and his shrieks changed into a child-like moaning. He did not utter wild sounds anymore and just stertorously whispered: "Bad, bad, bad."

Everybody around paused. Only the dog's howling interrupted the tense silence. Philip placed his hands on the giant's shoulders and looked into his eyes filled with tears.

"Did anybody hurt you, Karolek?" he asked in a soothing voice while talking very slowly. But Karolek just abruptly shook his head. At that moment, the dog again ruefully howled, and Philip got an idea:

"Did anything happen to Ivanko?"

Karolek's head nodded in wild agreement.

"And what happened to him, Karolek," Philip continued to ask.

Karolek did not answer. Only his moaning got stronger. Only after Philip repeated the question did he suddenly and abruptly pull the rope tied to Ivanko's dog, and then he stuck out his tongue, turned up his eyes, touched his throat, and raised the hand towards the sky. Then he started to weep wildly again.

Philip lowered his hands from Karolek's shoulders and turned over to several men who were not in the fields or vineyards that day and stood around with frightened faces.

"Ivanko hung himself," he said. "Go and find him and cut him down."

"Bad, bad," wailed the fool Karolek again.

But nobody paid any more attention to him. The street was filled with the excited talk of women who tried to compete with each other who knew more about the shepherd's life while trying to prevent children from joining the men. The men ran with whatever they had on up towards the bridge over the dried-up creek. Philip watched them as they disappeared in the curve of the road leading to the pastures behind the Wet Grove. Then he turned around and returned to the door of the store that was left open. But before he crossed the threshold, he looked up to Jacob who was standing there with the window on his shoulder and whose face was pale.

"Wait, I will join you."

He unfastened his apron, gave it to Chana, who still stood frightened in the door of the store, and walked slowly next to Jacob.

"Poor Ivanko," he said after a while, and Jacob who was quiet until now repeated after him:

"A poor man."

"Everybody has to hang his life on something at the end," Philip continued after a few steps. "One on God and the other on the noose." And when Jacob did not answer, he added: "He was a poor man. But he lost hope because he had more pity for himself than for others. A pitiful man."

Philip paused. He walked silently next to Jacob, but he noticed that he kept his eyes downcast whenever he glanced at him. When they reached the town square, they stopped.

"Goodbye, Jacob, I have to go back," Philip parted from him.

Jacob continued to look at the ground when he squeezed the offered hand. Only his lips uttered something that sounded like a whispered thanks.

After a few steps, Philip turned around. He saw Jacob with the window on his shoulder as he walked away. As if he felt Philip's gaze, he also stopped after a while and turned around. The old man waved at him. Then they both continued on their ways.

Chapter 16

Song about Pity

Daniel was bored for quite a while. In the morning, he argued with Jura Tomík, who did not play any other game besides cops and robbers, was always just bragging about something, and in general, was a dumb boy. And now, for more than half an hour already, he lingered in the kitchen where he bothered Chana with never-ending questions about what he should be doing.

When the bell on the door of the store rang, and Chana went out to check who was coming, Daniel sighted through the opened kitchen door the bulky stature of Uncle Jacob with the large window frame on his shoulder. He overheard Mother informing Jacob that Grandfather was in the workshop in the back. He also noticed that she raised the folding board between the two counters and took Jacob inside.

He rejoiced as the person of Uncle Jacob was in his childish mind connected with the image of kites Uncle Jacob made for him, with the birds he taught him to identify, and with the fish he taught him to catch. But only for a moment was he dazzled by that image before he recalled what they saw with David in the cottage up in the vineyards and what he overheard when he trailed behind Grandfather Philip and Grandfather Gabriel in Creekside Street. He wanted to run behind Uncle Jacob into Grandpa's workshop, where he liked to sit on the rocking chair with the netting that cracked with each swing. From that place, he liked to watch Grandpa's hands as they kneaded the putty and cut the glass. Sometimes, he even got a clod of putty that smelled like varnish and was allowed to roll out of it a puppet, a mushroom, or a bird. At other times, he coaxed from Grandpa pieces of glass or mirrors that he then used outside in the sun for dispatching a dancing fairy into the freckled face of Cousin

David. And once in a while, when Grandfather finished his work and wiped off his hands in the apron, he seated Daniel on the table customarily used for glazing and played Tick-Tack-Toe or checkers with him.

Even now, he would have liked to sneak through the store and slip into the workshop as when he thought about it, his grandfather and uncle were actually the two people whom he liked to listen to the most. But his recollection of the talk of both his grandfathers in the Creekside Street and of the sad face of Grandfather Gabriel with which he accepted Philip's offer that he would speak with Jacob was impressed deeply on his mind, and the boy revised his plans. He did not sneak behind Mother into the store but passed through the kitchen into the room where Grandfather usually slept along with his dog. Only the glass door covered with a light curtain separated him from the workshop. He crossed his legs and sat behind it on the floor while listening to the talk that penetrated there.

Dak, who slept nestled on the brown blanket on Philip's bed, blinked his lazy eyes, woke up for a moment from his nap, jumped down, waddled onto Daniel, and curled up between his legs. Daniel lightly squeezed his muzzle so that he would not betray him by barking. But Dak apparently did not think about anything like that and only quietly puffed into the boy's palm and, after a while, fell asleep again.

Daniel listened with one ear on the door while holding his breath so that he would not miss a word. He did not understand most of what Grandpa Philip was telling Jacob and was annoyed with himself for his foolishness. But he still grasped something. Grandfather said that it did not matter whether we believed that God existed or not. But it was essential to know that none of us would ever know that with a certainty. That meant, according to Grandfather, that we all were equally pitiful in our lack of knowledge and that because of it, we had to pity each other. That is how he seemed to explain it. Daniel was quite confused in his head from all of it, but repeated Grandfather's words to himself and tried to create a more coherent picture out of them.

We all are pitiful, Daniel repeated to himself. First, he recalled Kate, who did not get married because she limped. Yes, Kate is pitiful. And Mom is pitiful because Dad did not come back from the war. And Grandpa Gabriel is pitiful as he is suffering because of Uncle Jacob. And Uncle Jacob because he knows that what he does is not right but cannot help it. And widow Grün because she is poor. And all the farmers because the summer is dry, and the vineyards caught the blight. Oh yes, Grandpa Philip was right. All the people around, all of them, were pitiful – one for one reason and the other for another one. But Grandpa now said that they all were also equally pitiful because of something else.

Daniel recalled having a bad dream that scared him one time and woke him from his sleep. He dreamed that he was taking a stroll with his mother and that they entered a deep forest. They walked and walked until they got lost. They laughed at first, but then they gradually became more tired and more frightened. Twilight turned into a dark night, and they did not know where they were, or how to get out of the thick forest where one could only hear the hooting of the owls and the howling of the wolves. Their legs were exhausted, they stumbled over roots, their foreheads were hitting tree trunks, they were falling down but were always getting up again while trying to find the lost path. Whenever one of them was at the point of giving up, the other one supported and encouraged the other to search again. So they went and went through the endless forest until both of them started to weep, as they could not find a way out and a clearing in the woods was nowhere to be seen. In that dream, they embraced each other as they cried together. When he woke up, he pattered to Mother's bed and hid there under her quilt. And the next day he was really nice and helped in the kitchen by doing the dishes. He did not embrace Mom like in that dream but did everything she asked him without talking back. He liked her a lot as she, a poor woman, roamed the horrible woods with him during the night, could not find the way out, and had only him,

Daniel, as she held his hand.

Daniel recalled that dream when he tried to sort out in his head what Grandfather Philip said about all of us being equally pitiful because of our ignorance. Grandfather also noted that because of it, we had to have pity for each other. He also recalled how in his dream, he embraced Mother and suddenly felt that tears were filling his eyes, and he wanted to cry.

The first tears poured out of his eyes and ran down both his cheeks till they reached Dak's brown and warm back, shining like silk. The dog who was lying with his head leaning on Daniel's crossed legs just twitched his long ears as if he were trying to brush away a fly and continued to sleep.

Daniel recalled other tears and another forest where he wept because of equal pity. Because of the pity over the poor shepherd Ivanko who was one of the most pitiful.

At that moment, a terrible scream was heard from the street. It penetrated the walls and the door and reached through the store and Philip's workshop even there, to the back room.

Daniel jumped up and Dak, excited from the prolonged howling that joined the scream, started to bark as he ran with the boy through the kitchen and the hallway to the entrance door. Nobody noticed that Daniel's eyes were red from crying. They were all focused on Karolek as he hopelessly moaned in a voice that almost did not seem to be human while dragging behind him on a rope the ruefully howling shepherd's dog.

Then Grandfather, who stood in front of Karolek, lowered his hands from the giant's shoulders, turned to the nearby men, and said:

"Ivanko hung himself. Go and find him."

Daniel did not join the other children who were following the men running up to the pastures. He hid behind the door in the dark hallway, pressed his forehead to the wall, and bitterly started to weep. When the door opened again and Chana showed up, he turned abruptly and cuddled up to her like never before. Like only during that dream in the dark forest.

Chapter 17

Jacob

Jacob inserted the window into the frame and, without saying a word, slipped away from the house. He was glad that nobody saw him and that he did not have to talk to anybody.

He tottered out rather than walked out of the round entrance gate and hesitantly crossed the town square. He did not know yet where he would go. He wanted to see Helen. He had to see her. He had to touch her face to wake up from his daze. But the wave of shame inundated him again, and his legs were guided neither by reason nor by feelings but only by the clear sense of hopeless despair. He wanted to be alone again, he had to be alone, he had to grit his teeth, to scratch his nails in the bark of the nearest tree, and to nestle down into the firm ground that would not sink under his weight and that would allow him to put down roots and to grow. He made his decision, and his decision was firm. He will cut all the knots, break the walls that are choking him, and part from everything as everything was just a desert.

Only Helen was life.

And now Philip Taub, with only one breath, with only one word, caused the ground where he had anchored himself so firmly to start to cave in, to fall underneath his feet and to take him down deep into the abyss.

He did not turn left up to the road to the vineyards but went to the right, to the fields. He did not direct his steps but just walked wherever his legs carried him. At the white chapel with the picture of the Virgin Mary decorated with the dry bunch of corn poppy, he again made the right turn onto the narrow path that led to the river.

When he reached the water, he set out on the upstream trail around the bank of the slow stream. The air smelled of fish that once in a while emerged above the surface and then, with a heavy splash, fell back down into the water. In the bushes next to the other bank, two teals swam quietly, leaving behind them soft ripples that diverged behind their bodies into two weakening and gradually disappearing lines. The reed warbler flew up from the swinging stalk and, while staying close to the surface, disappeared somewhere in the bushes on the other side. Any other day Jacob would have watched all those things with joyfully enchanted eyes. But today, nothing was left from all that he usually experienced outside at the river, in the fields, in the meadows, or in the woods. Today, he did not understand the language of the fish and the birds and did not hear the pulse and breath of the trees. Nothing was left in his dulled and dazed head from what he used to accept as a sign of his fluttering and joyful God.

Like a sleepwalker, he placed one leg in front of the other, and step by step, he inched forward around the bank as if he did not have any spirit inside of him. But deep within, all of the restlessness of a hunted deer raged as he realized that the escape route from the hemmed-in circle was rapidly narrowing.

He did not even notice that he had passed the place where he met Helen for the first time, after so many years. But the long walk started to arouse in him a sense of discipline that had until now been hidden in a restless sleep on the hard bed of hopelessness, and his thoughts were becoming clearer. He suddenly realized that he had reached a crossroad. Should he choose the road leading to Helen, the pangs of conscience would never leave him. Should he come back, he would die from thirst in the desert. And there was no third way. But perhaps there is, perhaps yes. The words of Philip Taub about pity stuck in his mind like an invisible splinter that was hurting whenever a thought touched it. Pitiful, we all are awfully pitiful, Philip had said, as we were born into a timeless uncertainty. Because none of us will ever know, none of us will find the truth. But what did Philip Taub know about uncertainty? What could he know about the true pitifulness of a heart without any roots?

High above in the sky, a heron waved its wings. For a moment, it seemed to hang in place with its outstretched pinions as if it were crucified on the clouds. Then it flew quietly further away in the air. Jacob now shook off the shackles of his daze. He watched the receding bird. It is alone, so alone, he thought, and so free high in the skies without any crossroads. But then he heard the croaking of frogs in the reeds at the bank. Tomorrow, or perhaps even today, they will become the prey of one of those free birds.

Philip's words started to hurt him again. The pity, the overarching pity, that was Philip's remedy for all ailments. Perhaps he was right. To have pity inside of you. Maybe that truly solves all the mysteries. But didn't Jacob have pity inside of him? Didn't he have hundreds of various pities? Didn't he pity his father? Didn't he feel for his mother? Didn't he even pity Rebecca? The pity! Yes, the pity. There was not only one pity, but there were many pities, and it was necessary to weigh each of them separately and see which one was more important.

So let's think about those various pities, one at a time. His father came to mind first. Jacob's departure will inflict an even deeper wound in him than in his mother. What about Mother? In the end, that poor being was always able to reconcile with anything. She will even reconcile with losing another son. She will accept it as she has so far accepted everything humbly and bravely without a murmur. Only in her own corner, once nobody sees her, will she raise the tip of her apron and will weep. But she will accept it as a part of life against which a weak woman cannot fight. But what about Father? He will never understand and will never forgive. He will tear his clothes, mark his forehead with ashes, and sit shiva for the lost son. He will not be able to bear the shame brought by Jacob. He will not survive it as when he enters the synagogue, everybody will look at him, and their stealthy glances will speak: "Look, that is Gabriel Menasse. His son Jacob abandoned his own wife and ran away with some goyte. He raised him really well, didn't he? Pious Gabriel

Menasse! Really pious as he was not able to teach his son to pray and to fear God." Father will not survive it. He will even miss his work at the malthouse. But that is not the most important thing. It will be the shame that will kill him, the wounded pride, and the torture caused by searching for why his God, his strict but just God, is punishing him so harshly.

Mother, she will be patient. She will not cease walking around the house with her hands always ready to work and help. She will wait and will trust. She will trust without saying a word. She will trust that one day he will come back like she did not stop hoping that David would return from the war. And she will accept him without any reproach and will place a bowl of soup in front of him and will put him to bed like a child tired from wandering. But Rebecca? An unexpected blow will wake her up from sluggish lethargy. She will scold him, she will call down curses upon his head, she will run out crying into the street, perhaps she will be ruined, perhaps she will become insane, perhaps she will veil herself with the cloak of apathy and the features of her face will start to resemble those of her feeble-minded brother. Her face. The face he used to love. Where did all that love disappear, he thought, and again recalled the words of Philip Taub who said that love often disappeared but that pity, pity had to stay with us.

Yes, the pity. But why the pity for Rebecca and not the pity for Helen? Why the pity for the woman who drove him into suffocating suffering, and why not the pity for another woman in whose presence everything burst into bloom again? Did he leave Helen in doubt about his decision? Why should he have pity for Rebecca as next to her, his life was becoming crusty like a field without any rain? Why, why not the pity for Helen with whom he was joined in love? And next to her, he would wake up full of joy even if he had to live in poverty, even if he had to live from hand to mouth, and even if he had to go begging from house to house. If he came back, if he were still able to come back, wouldn't Helen be equally unhappy and equally pitiful as Rebecca will be once he leaves her?

He halted at the curve of the river where the small marshy bay was overgrown with reeds. He listened for a moment to the elegy of frogs and to the trembling of the stalks.

The pity, he said to himself and started to walk again. The pity. And what about pity for myself? Who has pity for me? Am I not poor? Do I not resemble the stalk of the reeds waving in the wind? Don't I have a right to have pity for myself? Should I bury my happiness because of pity for others? Whatever I do, somebody will be miserable. I already made it so far that there is no way back. I just have to decide who will suffer from pain. But if I must cause pain to somebody else regardless of what I do, why should I also hurt myself? It is true that if I leave with Helen, there will be a little shame and sadness in me for abandoning my home. And pangs of consciousness will show up once in a while. But if I suppress my memories, I will be happy. But can I force myself to not think about the mountain of pain I would leave behind? But if I stay, will not the pain in my heart be even bigger?

Why? Why should he think about others and not about himself? Why shouldn't he have pity for himself but should have pity for others? Philip did not provide an answer to that question. But was it not already answered by the shepherd Ivanko with the noose on the branch, up there in the Wet Grove?

Jacob did not know for how long he wandered on the curved path around the bank of the slow stream of the river. Even though he was not much wiser, his thoughts calmed down, and he felt that it was time to return. He turned around and followed the same route back home.

One thing became clear. No, his happiness was not the most important item in this game. Even though he felt that he was entitled to mercy from others, he could not pity himself. He would rather scold and accuse himself for ending up in a situation like that. He himself was at fault, only he himself was guilty. He made a mistake and deserved punishment. He deserved to suffer. He himself was surprised at how calmly he was able to contemplate his guilt and how clearly he understood that his own happiness was not at stake. He could not make a decision based on his happiness. He just had to consider carefully where there would be less pain, who would be able to carry it better, and who would break underneath its weight.

Even if for a moment he forgot about his father, Rebecca was here, and Helen was here too. They stood against each other in Jacob's mind. He tried to forget what each of them meant for himself but rather measured on a delicate scale the level of pain of both women. And together with the level of pain, a level of resilience too. Jacob suddenly got ideas that surprised him and slowed down his steps. A few moments ago, he was convinced that he could not live without Helen and that separation from her, that supreme sacrifice he would be making, would not only mean the end of his happiness but also the end of everything he called life. But he was further along now and asked himself which one of those two women could survive better without him. And answering that question led to a surprising conclusion that almost brought him to a standstill for a moment. Did he mean for Helen as much as she meant for him? If Helen were asked whether she would be able to live without Jacob, would her answer be as clear and firm as his? She for sure loved him. She provided him a lot of evidence for that, all the proofs only a woman can give a man. But didn't she live a fulfilled life even before they met, and couldn't she live equally fully even if he left tomorrow? The longer he thought about moments spent with Helen, the more confident he was that despite all their love, unlike him, Helen did not put the roots down yet. Tomorrow, she could raise the anchor and get on the move from the harbor she liked and in which she could stay forever but from which she could just as well embark on a journey to the open sea while seeking another safe haven. And Rebecca? In truth, she was perhaps more helpless, and only if he left her would she more fully realize what he meant for her and what she would be losing. But wouldn't she veil herself after an initial burst of hopelessness again with the cloak of an inert apathy? Wouldn't she build a fence of harshness around herself for protection from unpleasant memories, and wouldn't she live as if she had never met him?

At the moment Jacob asked himself that question, something stopped his steps completely. He remained standing as if suddenly dazzled by the stream of light. Until now, he felt as if he were crisscrossing through the dark room without windows and without any view. But now, as if some invisible hand had lifted the heavy curtain of fog, he could see again. The intense light hurt his eyes for a while before they were able to slowly adjust. No, Rebecca will not live like before as if she had never met him. A child will be here. Jacob's child, his own child. His child and her child. The child he was not thinking about, the child about whom he forgot, but who was at this critical moment pounding its tiny fist on the blinded window while announcing itself. It was not asking for its rights or love. It was not even begging for pity. But when Jacob thought about the child, everything was transformed into one large tear that did not well up in his eyes but spread through his blood and burned with each pulse through his vessels till it filled all the inner spaces of his heart.

As he stood in the open countryside, on the pathway around the bank of the river, he suddenly gained a clear understanding. How could he have not seen for a single moment? How could he have forgotten? He could leave his mother, he could reconcile with breaking his father's heart, he could abandon Rebecca, he could even sacrifice Helen, but how could he have even for a moment accepted that he could run away from his child? How could he look into its eyes? A feeling of shame before the unborn started to mix in his heart with pity for the helpless little being. Suddenly, two small reproachful eyes, not yet understanding what was happening but mirroring his shameful face, were the only things that were left. In front of those eyes, what was Jacob's happiness? What was the pain of others? Where their glance crossed Jacob's looks, in that intersection of reproach and shame, tenderness and pity, helplessness and responsibility, there was a point holding the heavy burden of life that had to be picked up and carried on his shoulders. Carried till the end. And carried joyfully and humbly and without a murmur. Jacob once again heard Philip Taub's words. "Whoever has enough pity will rather hurt himself. Who has pity in his heart carries life much easier."

Jacob now fully understood those words. He started to run. He did not look in front of himself as he rushed helter-skelter across the fields up to the vineyards. Now, now at this moment, he had to speak with Helen. Now, while he still wielded enough power, while he saw everything clearly, before the cover of uncertainty could fall on his feelings and cast a shadow on his decisions. He passed the chapel at the intersection and sprinted further up on the dusty road around the vineyards to the end of the slope where Helen's cottage stood. Then he breathlessly stormed inside.

"Helen!" he uttered in a hoarse voice. "Helen, where are you?"

Nobody answered. He ran in front of the house and around the vineyard, but Helen was nowhere to be found. He thus got back into the cottage and again entered the room. As when he was here for the first time, only half of the room was filled with sunlight. He now noticed for the first time that the window was shut. And he also noticed that in the middle of the room where the sunlight was turning into shadow, there was an oak table and, on the table, there was a glass jug that once was filled with flowers. And in front of the jug, there was a letter.

He grabbed it with his trembling hand, fiercely opened the envelope, and read. When he finished reading, he slowly sat down on the nearby chair.

So here it was. And he tortured himself. The suffering drove him mad and threatened to pile a lot of pain on others. But for Helen, as soon as an opportunity to become a little famous emerged, the theater started to dominate her life while Jacob faded away. Oh yes, Jacob recalled Professor Rohan, whom Helen had talked about in the past. "Listen to me, my girl – you've got some talent." Those words of praise made her really proud. And when Rohan wrote her now, she did not hesitate. Yearning for the lights of the stage and for the storm of applause forever overshadowed what Jacob had perceived as love.

So here it was. And Jacob sat on the chair, stared into space, and nodded his head like an old man. He suddenly felt tired after so much tension. He got up. His legs were like lead. But his heart felt surprisingly light and not as heavy as in previous days. In truth, it was still painful. But the pain was like the last thunder before the clouds tremble and a quiet and liberating rain starts pouring down.

He looked once more around the room. Here was the table where they used to sit. And here was the empty jug that once was filled with wildflowers. And over there, there was a sofa with a dark red blanket and a pink eiderdown cushion. And on the wall the portraits of pastor Garaj and his parents. Those pictures always somehow bothered him. He looked for the last time at the window and at the fleshy sunflower stalks around its frame. Then he got out on the road in front of the cottage and slowly walked back towards home. Now it was truly his home.

He descended down into the valley while calmly contemplating how oddly determined are the ways of human lives. Were they guided by God's wisdom? Or was it just a coincidence? We will never know. How right was Philip Taub! How pitiful are we! We all are equally pitiful! How not to have pity for human helplessness!

He reached the town and slowly passed through the tree-lined Creekside Street while focusing on his thoughts. When he reached its end and turned onto the narrow road leading to the town square, he met Spitzer, who was pushing a squeaky baker's cart with bread in front of him. When he noticed Jacob, he stopped his cart, and his oval face shined underneath his straw hat. He wiped his hands on his apron and waved at Jacob from a distance.

"Mazal tov," he called, "mazal tov!"

"Mazal tov?" Jacob did not understand why the old man was congratulating him.

"What? You do not know it yet? You do not know that you are a father? A son is waiting for you at home while you were wandering God knows where."

Jacob stood for a while. He could not believe what he was hearing. He had seen Rebecca in the morning, and it did not seem that her time would be coming soon.

"Why do you stand here like a block of wood? It came sooner than you had expected, didn't it? But do not worry about it. That happened to us too when Yitzchak was born."

But Jacob was not listening to him anymore. He started to run through the narrow road and soon vanished from Spitzer's sight behind the corner of the town square. The baker just shrugged his shoulders and said to himself: "Meshugge." Then he grabbed the cart again and pulled it further down the bumpy street.

Chapter 18

Salomon Rév

Summer was drawing to a close, and the days were getting shorter, allowing fall to cut their length like a shepherd shearing the sheep for their wool. And the time when the people would usually get ready to complete all the remaining farm work came, but this year was different. The farmers had already gathered all their poor harvest a long time ago. They were, however, unable to sow as the soil that was plowed with a lot of effort grew hard again like a stone, and the thick dry crust covered the fields, and the earth refused to accept the seed.

But in October, it started to rain again, and as if the skies were trying to make up for what they had missed, the water poured down for an entire week. All the peasants swarmed out into the fields and tried to quickly use that moment to sow. Then they waited while praying so that the seed would have enough time to sprout up and gain some strength before the earth cooled off and before the first cold winter nights came. But the earth, as if it tried to make up for its guilt, was doing its mighty work. Rapidly growing sprouts filled the sowers with new hope. Even in the vineyards, the plague halted its destructive march, and the blight stopped spreading, and the young sprouts grew up healthy and disease-free.

Life in town thus returned to its old tracks. Even though poverty did not leave its walls, it did not live there with despair anymore, but with hope. The nights were not filled with laments and curses anymore, but with expectations and prayers. Even Jacob, as if he had left the darkness, felt that the bitterness inside him was gradually making space for reconciliation. And Rebecca, as if revived over the cradle of their son, whom they named Philip as Philip Taub was his godfather, the sandek, during the circumcision ceremony, was less and less a dry desert during the day and more and more a blossoming orchard during the night. Even the shepherd's job was taken, and instead of unhappy Ivanko, the cows were now driven to the pasture by old Horvát who had lost his arm at the shoulder during the war. Only the elders of the kehilla felt under pressure as the new hope did not eliminate poverty, and the day when they had to separate from their holy Torahs and the holy treasure was getting relentlessly closer.

They promised each other to wait for the final decision until after the high holidays, but they all knew what the decision would be. But everybody agreed with Philip's suggestion as they all wanted to see their Torahs once more in all their beauty, covered in their white festive vestures. But the first day of the month of Tishri was getting closer, the day during which the New Year, Rosh Hashana, is celebrated. The day was only separated by eight days, the eight most holy days of the year, from the highest holiday, the Day of Atonement, or Yom Kippur, the day with the holiest day-long fast.

For the entire week before New Year's Day, shammash Rév's wife and Timfeld's long-legged maid wiped every corner of the shul, and shammash Rév assigned jobs to all his six children and personally made sure that everything was clean and shining. Then, a day before the actual holiday, he brushed his clothes, smoothed his rusty-red beard, and while reciting the words of the prayers, he approached with his washed hands the receptacle with the holy Torahs. He pulled the cord used for opening the curtain from the red velvet and turned the key in the door behind which the sacred scrolls of the Torah were kept. Then he took each of them out separately and brought them to the altar from which tomorrow the whimpering tenor of the cantor will announce the day is near for when we are to appear in front of God and account for our deeds in front of the Supreme Judge. And then he dressed each scroll into the vesture from the snow-while silk and red velvet embroiled in gold with the name of God. On the top of the wooden cylinders on which the sacred scrolls of parchment were rolled up, he attached the silver crowns, *Rimonim*, decorated with tiny bells. On the top of each Torah, he then hung using a silver chain a shining wrought shield Tas with the sign of lions of Judah, and a silver pointer yad that will be used tomorrow by the person reading from the Torah so as to not lose his place while reading the Torah portion. When he was done with his work, he once more walked around the entire room. He touched each pew and each candelabra with his finger to make sure that not a speck of dust was left there, and then with one hand behind his back and the other on his rusty-read beard, he stopped in each corner to search for spiderwebs. He then poured additional oil into the ever-burning Ner Tamid light hanging above the Ark of the Covenant, replaced the red velvet curtain with the while silk one, closed it, and once he was finally satisfied, left the shul. Then he crossed the courtyard and entered the small house with two rooms, standing behind the shul, where every shammash of this kehilla lived with his family since time immemorial.

It was late afternoon, the festive evening prayer was to start in an hour, and several tasks still needed to be accomplished. It was necessary to wear over regular clothes a white shroud kittel in which he will be one day buried and in which on this day of judgment he has to stand in front of God. It was necessary to get a white cloth ready into which the ram's horn, shofar, will be wrapped that will be used by wagoner Fischer to summon for the supreme judgment. And it was necessary to wish his wife *leshana tova tikateivu* so that all her prayers would be answered and so that she would be inscribed in God's books for a good year ahead. The shammash, who has a lot of work to do even on these holidays, would have no time after the prayers, like everybody else, to give his wife the traditional new years greeting.

So after he put the on the kittel and kissed his wife and

children, he came back to the synagogue. He removed the shofar, the twisted ram's horn, from the cabinet behind the altar, where cups and receptacles with spices *besamim* and other liturgical items were stored. Then he wrapped it in the white cloth he brought with him from home and placed it on the altar. Next, he checked his pew at the wall next to the entrance and put the book with Rosh Hashana prayers in front of him. Once he finished getting everything ready, he left his pew and stood next to the door to greet the first congregants and wish them all the best and that all their prayers would be answered.

Just before six o'clock, they started to gather. They came dressed in festive clothes and in a festive, but solemn mood. They came with their wives and older children, hugged each other and greeted each other:

"Leshana tova tikateivu."

"Let all your prayers be answered."

"May you be inscribed for a good year ahead."

And at the door, shammash Rév shook everybody's hand somewhat like a host and wished everybody:

"Leshana tova, leshana tova, leshana tova tikateivu."

All the women entered the side room which was next to the actual prayer room but was not connected to it with the door but instead with two window openings that narrowed towards the male section of the shul. The men gathered there and sat in their pews. Some of them were putting on their white kittels. They all placed their prayer books in front of them and greeted Rabbi Kupfer, who looked, with his full black beard, even more dignified than usual, and cantor Hercka who walked from pew to pew and shook everybody's hand. They were all already here. Rosh Hakol Timfeld and butcher Beinhacker sat in their seats at the opposite ends of the first row of pews. In his kittel, wagoner Fischer stepped around and coughed nervously as the uneasy task of blowing the shofar awaited him in the next day's morning service. Philip Taub whispered to his neighbors Gabriel Menasse and baker Spitzer. In the pew behind them, tinsmith

Kahan explained something to textile merchant Samuel Klein, and brush maker Tolnai was tapping soothingly on the shoulder of the constantly worried tailor Šefránek. Traveling salesman Kantůrek tried to use the last moments to not forget to wish Happy New Year to everybody, and in order to not miss anybody, he followed the cantor from pew to pew. Teacher Lebenhart looked even more seedy than usual tonight as the New Year's Eve did not offer any reasonable opportunity for getting bitter, and his gall bladder thus did not work. Jacob, Moshe, and Ruben Menasse stood quietly in the pew behind their father. The boys David and Daniel squeezed between them, repeatedly looked at the back pew where shammash Rév's sons sat and where wagoner's boy Isi, tall like his father, together with Guyla and Moshe Šefránek tried to push and shove from the edge of the bench fat Žigo Kantůrek, who weighed twice as much as his father. All the kehilla was there, including the feeble-minded son of tinsmith Kahan, and they were just waiting for the first star to come out in the sky.

Then shammash Rév approached the curtain covering the Ark of the Covenant, drew it, and opened the door. All the Torahs in their white shining festive vestures were seen. Hercka's whining voice resonated through the congregation, and everyone stood up and fell silent.

Shammash Rév's eyes fondled every section of the snow-white vestures covering the Torahs, and his mind touched each shining ornament that he used for decorating the scrolls for the time of holiday period. Only one more week, he said to himself and nodded his rusty-red beard. Only a few more days and this would all be gone. That will be the end, he repeated to himself as he retreated to his pew that was just at the synagogue entrance from where he could have a view of the entire synagogue interior. The end. He will not be able to hold each Torah in his hands, he will not dress them in the vestures embroiled in gold, he will not decorate their heads with crowns with silver bells, he will not hang wrought Mizrachs on them. The end.

He kept thinking about it as he passed absent-mindedly from the altar to the cabinet with the Torahs and then back again to his pew at the entrance. For the shammash, holidays meant work, and shammash Rév never served God more lovingly and more humbly than right on high holidays. But this day, he knew that his heart was not focused on the service. Again and again, he caught himself not thinking about the words of the prayers, and it was for the first time ever that he forgot to leave his pew on time to close the curtain in front of the ark with the holy scrolls. The cantor had to angrily look at him with blazing eyes from the altar. But was it his fault? He tried to focus only on the holiness of the day, but, painfully, his mind could not adore the kehilla's treasured Judaica items behind the white curtain, without being reminded of what would happen in just a week. One more week. One more week and the cabinet will become empty, and all the glitter and all the glory and all the beauty will be gone.

Curled up in his pew, his eyes roved about the words of the prayers in the book that was open in front of him, but deep inside his heart, another prayer was rising, a prayer that was never written and never pronounced until now.

I know, said the heart of shammash Rév, that this is the day of your glorious judgment, my Lord. I know that on this day, it is inscribed in your books who will rise up and who will go down, who will die and who will live, who will live his days in joy and who in sadness, who will live in poverty and who in abundance. You, my Lord, know that Salomon Rév is the humblest among your servants and that he always accepted your judgment without any grumbling. But it is also written that the pity that reaches your ear may change your judgment. And only for that reason, I beg you, my Lord, to spare Salomon Rév this humiliation. All that is meant to happen next week is happening only to save the job of myself, the rabbi, and the cantor so we and our children will not perish from hunger. Give me, my Lord, different service, and I will take my wife and my children, and we will go wherever you lead us. But where? Where should we go? Where should I search for bread for my children? Tell me, my Lord, who blessed the womb of my wife so that our family grows almost every year. I know that I have no right to beg you for a miracle. Why should you perform miracles just for Salomon Rév? But I am still asking you, my Lord, for a miracle before Braun from Břeclav comes and pays the price that will give me bread, the bread that I will never be able to swallow without bitterness.

So shammash Rév talked to the Lord, and the feeling that the good God was somewhere listening to what he did not even whisper aloud took the weight of despair off his heart. In truth, he was only speaking for now while God, the Lord of hosts, remained covered in clouds of silence. But can God leave requests from his humblest servant without an answer?

At that moment, shammash Rév calmed down and started to pay more attention to the service again. Cantor Hercka just sang the verse from the Psalm:

"May only goodness and kindness pursue me all the days of my life, and I will dwell in the house of the Lord for length of days."

The heart of shammash Rév felt much lighter as he sensed that he overheard in those words a promise from God.

His frail body, dressed in his kittel, that white shroud, was regularly swaying back and forth like a branch waving under the gusts of wind, and his rusty-red beard resembled a bloody autumn leaf tossed between earth and heaven by a November storm. He waited at his place in the pew next to the door for a moment, even after Rabbi Kupfer gave his final blessing to the congregation. Then, as if suddenly awoken from a dream, he jumped from his pew to the door so that he could open it before people started to leave. He smiled at everybody, bowed in front of everybody, and again humbly wished everybody: "Leshana tova tikateivu."

The synagogue was slowly becoming empty. In the hallway in front of the door and in the courtyard, they all once more shook each other's hand and exchanged best wishes. But women, they rushed back home so that they could prepare the festive dinner.

Shammash Rév stood in front of the entrance and waited until everybody left. Then he watched as Timfeld's maid extinguished candles at the altar and the prayer pews, and once it was done, he asked her to turn the key in the lock and to bring it to him to the house behind the synagogue.

Over there, Rachel, in the meantime, prepared dinner. They sat around the table with the white tablecloth. But before Rachel brought the meal, shammash Rév, as if by accident, moved the plate and pretended to be surprised once he found underneath it a letter written, like in previous years, by his sons. In the letter, his sons thanked him for all he gave them in the past year and promised to behave well and work hard in the upcoming year. As he seemed to be deeply touched, Rachel already placed before them on the table a bowl with a mixture of pears, carrots, and cabbage with sugar. In addition to this sweet fodder called tzimmes, she offered them a slice of apple dipped in honey and wished them to have the year ahead as sweet and tasty as this meal. But before they started to eat, Rachel walked around the table and placed into everybody's mouth a bite from the head of the fish so that they all would be the first in whatever they did in the upcoming year.

At the end of the dinner, the sons of shammash Rév approached him one by one, kissed his hand, and wished him a good night. He lifted his hands up with his eyes closed, placed them over their heads, and said the words of blessing. At that time, he felt not like the poorest of the kehilla, like a synagogue servant, but like a king with immense and immeasurable treasures.

There were no dark tomorrows anymore. There was only a beautiful today and a glorious, clear, and shining day after tomorrow.

Chapter 19

Spitzer

It became a tradition that on Friday between the holidays of Rosh Hashana and Yom Kippur, baker Spitzer was invited for dinner at Philip's house. They did not deviate from that unwritten rule even now though Chana had to implement all her thriftiness and all her culinary arts every week to convert their low supplies into at least half-full plates. But even if the table remained half-empty, the Friday evening was the Friday evening. Even if they had to starve the entire week, the evening of Shabbat had to be welcomed and celebrated like the entrance of the bride into the bridegroom's house with the white tablecloth, lighted candles in candelabras on the table, with the braided Sabbath bread, *barches*, with a sip of the wine, and an aroma of spices.

Through all the days of poverty, Philip always insisted that his destitution would not change how he acted in front of God and the people. And he expected the same from his loved ones. It even happened one day that Dak stole the bone hidden underneath the table in the butcher's shop and brought it back home. At that time, Philip, for the first time, hit Dak, took away the bone, wrapped it in paper, and he himself went to the butcher's store to return it. And while there, he again gave Dak, who apologetically followed him, an unpleasant scolding, and as a punishment, the dog was not allowed to go out with him for the next two days.

So strictly insisted Philip that poverty could not change any of his accepted rules, and one of those rules was that baker Spitzer was invited twice per year for dinner since the day his wife passed. Once for the glorious seder supper, on the eve of Pesach, and for the second time on Friday between Rosh Hashana and Yom Kippur holidays. On that evening, Spitzer joined Philip as they walked together from the evening prayer service at the synagogue and did not have time to stop at home before that.

It thus happened that he was not aware of the letter that was delivered that evening to his house by old Ferenčák. In the morning, when the baker went together with Philip like every other day to the morning prayer service, Ferenčák, like always, just waved his hand above his head, and Spitzer shrugged his broad shoulders in disappointment. But then during the day, a thick letter with an American stamp arrived, and though it was already getting late and it was time to put away his drum and to get with his saber in front of Kohút's pub to maintain order, he instead armed himself with the mailman's knapsack and brought the letter to Spitzer's house. He looked inside through the window and saw the kerosene lamp lit up as the neighbor Mrs. Tymeš always lighted it for the baker on Friday evenings. He then knocked in vain on the gate but nobody showed up. He just begrudgingly left the letter under the door and walked away to assume his bailiff's duties.

Thus, baker Spitzer found the mail for which he had waited for so many months once he returned home from the dinner at Philip Taub's place. Initially, when he entered the dark hallway, he had not seen it. But once he opened the door to the room where the lamp was burning, and once he tried to close it behind him, something white was visible at the end of the beam of light on the floor at the edge of the entrance gate, and his heart started to beat with anticipation. He bent down, picked up the letter, and rushed with it towards the light. But when he was getting his trembling fingers ready to open the thick envelope, he suddenly dropped the letter on the table and remained standing as if he were stunned.

It was Friday evening. Shabbat started a while ago, and it was a sin to do anything which resembled work. To lighten the light, strike the match, and replenish the fire, that all was a sin. He had already sinned when he picked up the letter from the floor. And now, he would have almost committed another sin if he had tried to tear the edge of the envelope that separated him from what he was waiting for, for so long.

He ran very excited out of the house and knocked on the gate at Tymešes, his neighbors. He waited for a moment and then knocked again, but nobody came to open it. After he drummed with his fingers on the downstairs window and nobody responded, he recalled that Mrs. Tymeš mentioned in the morning that they might go to Vrádiště to visit their daughter and that they might stay there overnight.

Disappointed, he returned home, sat at the chair next to the table, and for a long time focused directly on the white rectangle of the thick envelope that laid in front of him. So Yitzhak finally wrote. He did not forget. His Yitzhak did not forget. But what did he write? Is he sending only belated Rosh Hashana wishes? But why is the envelope so thick? He touched it timidly with his fingers, examined it from all the sides as if he was trying to feel what was hidden inside. Yitzhak is probably sending pictures of the children, he thought. How do they look like, his beloved darlings? Oh my Lord, why couldn't it arrive a day earlier?

He did not know how long he just sat there while looking in front of him at the letter on the table. Only the loud and rattling chimes of the old clock on the wall reminded him of how late it already was. It was too late to get out to try to wake up somebody who could open the envelope for him. They would not understand. And they would get angry. And to cause anger is also a sin. With a heavy heart, he got up from the table and dragged himself to bed.

But sleep did not visit him that night. He tossed and turned from side to side, moaned, and often opened his eyes impatiently to check for the first glimmer of the morning light. The night seemed to be endless. The temptation to get up and open the envelope was present all the time, but he was always able to suppress it. You walked all your life in fear of the Lord, he said to himself, why couldn't you break the law just once? Nobody would get hurt, nobody would know about it, and merciful God would for sure forgive such a small sin of the impatient father, such as opening the envelope during Friday night. But every time, he replied to himself: Don't we sin enough even without our knowledge? Are we allowed to knowingly add to the bag of our sins even one more?

So he was tormented and tossed himself back and force almost till the sunrise when he fell asleep due to exhaustion. But the horn of shepherd Horvát that sounded from the corner of the road after half-past four, the squeaky crackle of the opening gates from which walked cows with a rolling gait and prolonged lowing on their daily way to the pastures, finally woke him up. He jumped from his bed like a young boy, quickly dressed up, and ran out into the street.

On the opposite side of the road, Mrs. Kazbunda was just closing the gate behind her heifer. Spitzer grabbed the peasant woman's hand and dragged her across the street to the table with the letter. She got mad and grumbled about the old fool, but Spitzer did not pay any attention. With the glasses in wire frames on the tip of his nose, he became engrossed in the crooked lines of his son's handwriting, and even if the good-natured neighbor threw flames at his face instead of swearwords, he would not have noticed it. A bliss that spread out on his oval face was just a weak reflection of the happiness that penetrated his entire being.

Three photographs and a bundle of dollar banknotes fell from the envelope onto the table. But the old man grabbed the letter first and delved into the reading. So that is how it was. Yitzhak, his Yitzhak wrote to him. He wished a happy New Year to his father and talked about his children on two sheets densely covered with crooked and crude handwriting. His older one, Sami, had already started school, and he himself will soon be thus able to write to his grandfather. The younger Nathan had measles recently but fully recovered by now and looks quite strong again, as you can see in the enclosed pictures. He then detailed the successes of his bakery, but then, the most important section came. Yitzhak always wanted his father to join them so that they could live happily together. And now he had made enough money, and his life became more secure, which meant that Father would not need to work and could just rest and only enjoy his grandchildren. In truth, he could always use help from such a good baker in his bakery but shouldn't his father just relax and leave the struggles to the younger ones? In fact, he wanted to come for his father by himself, but he cannot abandon the business for so long. That is why he is sending some money for the journey and the address of the travel agency. Once Father sorts out his affairs at home, he just needs to write to that address, and they will reserve a spot for him on the nearest ship. Rivka and both boys are already looking forward to meeting their grandfather. Just look at the attached pictures and see how well his grandsons are doing and how smart they seem to be, and that will prompt him to join them as soon as possible.

Spitzer removed the glasses from his moist eyes, wiped them with the edge of the tablecloth, then he put them back on the tip of his nose and looked at the photographs lying on the table next to the bundle of the banknotes.

On the first one was little Nathan with a head of curly hair and a wide smiling face that seemed to be more oval than the ball he held in front of him in his chubby hands.

On the second one was Sami dressed as a sailor with the school backpack on his back and the tablet from slate in his hand, with one leg stepping forward and looking as if he was getting ready to conquer the world.

On the third one was the entire family. Yitzhak and Rivka sat on the beautifully carved bench. They both had festive clothes, Rivka's hand was wrapped around Sami's neck, and she smiled blissfully. Yitzhak had little Nathan on his lap, but he sat so that the thick chain on father's vest would be visible, and with a happy smile on his cheeks, his head looked up from the high and stiff collar. The old man took, again and again, each photograph into his hands, took off his glasses, and placed the pictures close to his eyes, but then he put the glasses back on and again started to read Yitzhak's letter. But he did not touch the bundle of banknotes and did not even count them as it was Shabbat, and to handle the money would belong among the gravest sins.

After spending a long time reading and dreaming over the pictures, he realized that it was already morning, and noticed that the little hand on the clock on the wall almost showed seven o'clock. He quickly got up from the table, changed his clothes, put a broad-brimmed straw hat on his head, and rushed to the corner on Creekside Street where he waited every morning for Philip Taub.

But this morning, he had to wait longer than usual as the impatience that pushed him to share the good news with his friend led him to the place where they would meet much sooner today. But once Philip with Dak came nearby with his small hasty steps, Ferenčák, with the postal knapsack over his shoulder, appeared in the opposite direction. But this time he did not wave his hand above his head as he used to, but before the baker could say anything to Philip, Ferenčák yelled at him from a distance:

"Mr. Spitzer, have you found that letter yesterday? Where were you wandering?"

"I found it. I found it, thanks a lot," the baker replied across the street, somewhat disappointed that he could not share it with Philip by himself first, but on the other end was also happy that the news had already got out.

"So Yitzhak wrote? You see, I told you that it would come. Mazal tov, mazal tov! And what does he write?" Philip beamed with joy from Spitzer's happiness.

And Spitzer told and retold again once they reached the town square and in the window of the second house from the corner, the angular face of Gabriel Menasse appeared after Philip knocked on the glass.

"So well, he wrote," Gabriel uttered when they turned at the end of the side road towards the synagogue. Miracles still happen. Sometimes you get respect and gratitude from your children, he thought. But he forced out of himself only a quiet "mazal tov." And even that seemed to be almost strangled as if it was not able to pass his throat. Once they reached the oval opening in the white wall around the synagogue, he added:

"So you will leave us."

It sounded like half a question and half a statement of reality with which they had to become reconciled. But Spitzer rather heard in it pity and reproach, and at that moment, he for the first time fully realized what Yitzhak's letter really meant.

He did not answer and, without saying a word, entered behind the others into the synagogue and sat down in his pew. With learned and accustomed movements, he covered himself in his tallit, kissed its fringes, his trembling lips whispered a prayer, and his body started to rock in a rhythm, from side to side and also at times back and forth. But all of that was what his fingers, mouth, and body used to do every day since his childhood. But his mind was somewhere else today.

He sat down or got up from his spot based on the importance of the prayer led by the cantor's moaning voice. He knew every word, every syllable, and knew when the cantor would raise his voice as if searching for a crack through which his request would reach heaven, and when he would cut the sentence short as if throwing it into the wind which would bring the plea close to God's ear. While his lips whispered memorized prayers, his mind did not pay any attention to them but was turning around events from the past that appeared clearly in front of his eyes, not veiled in the fog of ancient times. He saw himself as a young boy at his bar mitzvah when he was called for the first time to the altar to read from the Torah and thus became a man and a member of the kehilla. He saw himself in front of the same altar the day after he brought Rosa into his home – my Lord, how beautiful she was – he came into this holy assemblage to hear the mazal tov that had loudly resonated from all the corners. And then there was a bar mitzvah of his sons when everybody came to shake his hand and touch his shoulder, and everybody wished him a lot of joy from his sons. But in this pew where he sat today, as on the other days with his face turned towards the East, he also heard the words of condolences and sympathy at the time when God took away his Rosa – why did she have to leave so soon? – and then again once he learned that Nathan was killed on the front.

He saw all those moments, joyful and also sad, all those moments and many more clearly before his eyes. But at that point, shammash Rév approached his pew so that he would deliver to him *aliyah shlishi,* announcing that on this Shabbat, he was honored by being asked to approach the Torah as the third one and to read the section from the Scripture that was assigned to him. It was difficult for him to interrupt his recollections and dreaming, and once his turn came, he faltered and stumbled like never before as the glasses on his eyes became moist, and his voice spoke hesitantly from emotion and often rambled from excitement. When he returned to his pew to make space in front of the altar for Abeš Tolnai, others greeted him as always with loud "*Yasher Koach,*" but he did not reply to them. Today he did not know where to look and was relieved once he sat down at his place.

While there, he stealthily gazed from underneath his glasses at pew after pew, stopped at each person, and tried to recall what he knew about them, what he ever talked to them about, and what shared memories they had. Then his eyes wandered over every corner and over every crack in the wall he knew about. He got up in his pew, and his body started to rock in harmonic movements back and forth, back and forth, while his eyes focused on the velvet veil covering the altar in front of which stood Tolnai who read from the open Torah. Perhaps it was the one from which he himself read so many years ago during the celebration of his bar mitzvah. Maybe Yitzhak or poor Nathan read from that same Torah when they turned thirteen. Today was the Saturday before Yom Kippur, and next week Braun from Břeclav will come again, and the kehilla will have to part with their most valuable Torahs and other treasures. Braun had named his price, and they all knew that they could not get more. The day after tomorrow is the Long day, and Braun had named his price. It is a sin to ponder about money on the Shabbat and even in the synagogue, but Spitzer, despite trying hard, could not prevent his mind from wandering in that direction. Others, for sure, had similar thoughts. But Spitzer, at the same time saw in front of him a bundle of dollar banknotes that he left on the table in his house. He had not even counted them. But was their value so much less than what Břeclav's Braun was willing to pay?

He attempted to push that thought away, but it came back with persistent obtrusiveness. He forced his lips to loudly recite the hymns instead of whispering, and his body started to rock in longer swings. But waves of doubts were, again and again, eroding the soft and loose bank of his decisiveness. For how long has he waited for Yitzhak's letter? For how many years has he not thought about anything else than about the moment when he would conclude all his affairs here and depart far away to his son with whom he will spend the rest of his days. And now, when that moment came, now, when he simply has to pack, shake everybody's hand, and embark on the journey, now his eyes suddenly wander over each crack in the wood of his pew while he stealthily gazes from underneath his glasses at all the faces around him while saying to himself: I am supposed to abandon all of this.

His body rocked like a tree tossed around by gusts of wind, but somewhere deep inside of him, an even more violent storm was raging. Something threatened to uproot the trunk, but its roots were rooted too deep in the soil and tried to resist, and the trunk and its branches were cracking under pressure. Nobody knew what was happening in the heart of Ya'acov Spitzer at that moment. Nobody knew about the rack on which all the limbs of his soul were painfully stretched as his lips recited the words of prayers as usual, like for so many decades. He himself was not aware even yesterday how deep his roots were and how deep his connection was to everything here around him. It was not until today that he realized that he was not like the ships that can drop and lift their anchor wherever and whenever they feel like it, but more like ancient trees covered with moss that forgot about their roots and recalled them only at the moment when a storm threatened to tear up their trunk. Far behind the sea, Yitzhak and his grandchildren waited for him and, together with them, a well-earned rest without any additional worries. But could he abandon all this here? Could he just pack his stuff, say goodbye, and never come back? Could he leave, was he allowed to leave, and did he want to leave?

Hercka sang the last Shabbat hymn, and the rabbi blessed the congregation with his raised-up arms holding the fringes of the tallit. They rose up in their pews, waved at each other, wished to each other *Git Shabes*, good Shabbat, and walked towards the exit. Even shammash Rév left his spot, stood at the door, and wished to each member separately: "Git Shabes, Git Shabes." But baker Spitzer still remained seated in his pew. Now, when his lips stopped whispering the learned words of prayers, the uncertainty inside of him shook him even more forcefully.

Once he roused himself, he shuffled behind tailor Šefránek, who was the last to leave. He walked mechanically around the shammash and hardly thanked him for his greeting. He did not even chat with Philip in the courtyard, as was their custom, and did not wave at anybody. He wanted to be left alone. He had to be alone. What did they know about his worries? He kept his hands behind his back while his head fell between his broad but sinking shoulders. His eyes, still wearing his glasses as he forgot to remove them, turned down to the ground. And he ordered his legs, twisted after years of work at the oven, to carry him back home.

Chapter 20

Daniel

Daniel could not stop worrying. He could not push it out of his mind. An icy fright drifted at him from the crack through which he was able to peep into the world of adults, for the first time in the forest behind the Wet Grove and then again behind the window of the priest's cottage in the vineyards. Full of fear but also pity, he repeated to himself again and again what he learned. There are no devils, but there are evil people who hurt the good ones, and nobody, not even God, is punishing them for it. He did not understand what had happened with Uncle Jacob. It was undoubtedly evil too. Everything that had to be kept secret was evil, and Aunt Rebecca for sure did not know about it and will hopefully never learn about it. There were evil things that people could correct on their own. But there were also other ones against which they were helpless and which could be punished only by God.

Daniel knew that since his new cousin was born, something changed in the hearts of Uncle Jacob and Grandfather Gabriel. Whenever he visited his grandfather, he looked up from the holy book he was reading and smiled at him. And when Daniel asked Uncle Jacob once about his new cousin, he was the same again like in the past. "He is growing," he said, "he grows up really fast. Soon we will go fishing together." And he laughed and was again as friendly to Daniel as before, and he really liked it. But that one who stole Margita from Ivanko was evil and remained unpunished. Why, he asked again like that time, why don't you, my God, punish that evil man?

Since the death of Ivanko, he could not think about anything else. He did not wish for anything more than just punishment for the evil man who stole the wife from Ivanko and later killed him.

Punishment, punishment, that word was always ringing in his ears. He was full of it, but there was nobody around with whom he could speak about it. With nobody except God Himself. He could speak to Him but would not get any answers.

Punish him, my Lord, he prayed. Punish him now, at this moment. I want to believe that you are just and that you punish the evil ones. If I could, I would go to kill him myself. But I do not even know who he is or where to search for him. But you know. You know everything, and it is your duty, my Lord, your task, to protect and reward the good ones and to search for the evil ones and to punish them. Punish him, my Lord, so that I would believe that you are just. Punish him so that I would know that you exist. That you really exist.

He felt shaky inside as he realized how frightening his request was, but despite that, repeated it again and again. And the anger at God who did not answer was boiling inside of him more and more.

Even now, late in the afternoon, he could not chase away that thought. Philip had no more work in his workshop, but as he always had to do something, he sorted the goods on the shelves in the store. Other times, the boy liked to watch him, followed Philip everywhere, and helped him to straighten rolls of the linen so that they would really be in line like lined-up soldiers. He handed to grandfather whatever he needed, he climbed behind him on the ladder and tried to be helpful. Today, however, he hid together with Dak behind the counter, stretched out on his back, and with his hands behind his head, he looked into the twilight and repeated for at least a hundred times already his prayer.

Perhaps God is already old, he thought. Maybe He does not hear very well anymore like Abeš Tolnai, and it is necessary to tell him everything multiple times before he understands it. He would prefer to cry out his request as loud as he could, but it was, of course, not possible. It was between God and himself, and nobody else was allowed to hear it. He thus whispered again and again: "Please punish him, my Lord, punish him, punish him!"

He repeated it in his mind even when the bell above the entrance to the store rang. Wagoner Fischer, the beanpole whose voice Daniel immediately recognized even without seeing him, entered the room. Dak ran out and wagged his tail to greet the guest, but Daniel remained in his hideout in the twilight behind the counter.

The wagoner loudly apologized for coming so late, but he had just returned from Skalica and only needed something minor. The lantern from the rear of his wagon broke, and he just came to ask Philip to cut new glass for it. And while Philip was working on it, the wagoner shared what he saw in Skalica today.

Twice per year, it was necessary to take the municipal bull there so that his health could be checked. Otherwise, they would have to call for a veterinarian, and it would cost much more, and the municipality tried to save money wherever possible. Until Ivanko's death, it was the task of the former shepherd. Today, the bull was taken for the first time by the new shepherd. He led him on the chain, all the way through the Wet Grove to Skalica, but once he reached the town, he wanted to wash the dust out of his throat. He tied the bull up to the tree in front of the lower pub and left for a small drink. And Fischer was at the same place quenching his thirst with a pint of cold beer.

Suddenly, it was possible to hear the sound of a trumpet and a drum roll, and they all ran out of the pub. Everybody wanted to see the parade of comedians announcing that the circus was coming to town and inviting the public for an evening performance. Two white horses were ridden by a half-naked Indian and by a white Esmeralda who was blowing kisses with her hands all over the place. Next to them ran several jesters with drums, trumpets, and cymbals. A young woman in tight clothes led a dancing bear on a chain, and in front of her walked a muscular giant on whose shoulders stood a Lilliputian with a monkey sitting on his head. However, in front of the parade was a man in a red leotard, a juggler, throwing up five red balls and then catching them back in his hands, while from time to time bowing to spectators who started to gather and were lining the road.

But they did not admire the colorful parade for long. Irritated by the red color of his leotard, the bull suddenly broke away from his chain, and with his horns tilted down, he dashed forward towards the juggler. The horses carrying the half-naked Indian and the white showgirl bolted, and even the frightened bear stampeded away and dragged behind him the pretty trainer. The monkey jumped off the Lilliputian's head, the dwarf from the giant's shoulders, and they all, together with the jesters, who lost their humor, ran away from the furious bull. However, the bull was thrusting the sharp horns repeatedly into the writhing body of the man in the red leotard.

The guys in front of the pub and on the edges of the road stood for a moment as if frozen. Once they started to move, they grabbed rakes and shovels, chains and buckets with water, and finally defeated the bull, whose anger had meanwhile diminished. But the man lying in the puddle of blood did not show any signs of life.

Fischer finished his story, but Philip did not say a word. God knows what he is doing, he thought as he often did before, but he did not know what to tell. There was silence for a while, and one could only hear the hissing of Philip's diamond on the smooth surface of the glass.

But the silence was interrupted by a heartbreaking scream. Daniel leaped, as if bitten by a snake, from his hideout, fiercely rushed out of the store, and a long-drawn-out painful wail waved behind him like a banner of despair.

Chapter 21

All is Well

Daniel ran out of the store, then passed through the hallway to the small room behind grandfather's workshop, fell on the couch, turned towards the wall, and while covering his eyes with his hands, he wept bitterly. The imploring scream escaping out of his throat when he had listened to Fischer's account changed into sobbing, but he was still trembling.

"O my God, what happened to you?" Chana came running up to him from the kitchen. She touched his forehead and his cheeks and said fearfully: "The child has a fever."

His teeth chattered, and he started to shiver from the fever. Even Philip came, held his hand, lifted up his chin, and looked straight into his eyes.

"Something happened to you?" he asked. But Daniel lowered his eyes, shook his head, his teeth were chattering, and he could not stop crying. He did not even resist when they half led him, and half carried him into the room where his bed was.

I killed him, he was saying to himself, I killed him, I killed that man. It was me who killed him, not the bull. He was only sent by God to carry out the punishment so that I would believe that he was just. If I had not asked for his punishment, he would live now. I killed him. I killed him. Why, my Lord, why did you listen to my stupid requests? I already know that you are just. But why did you just listen to me? Why did you not punish him in a different way? Why did I have to kill him?

Chana, who was running around him like a frightened mother hen, removed his clothes, laid him onto the bed, put socks soaked in the vinegar on his hot feet, covered him under a thick eiderdown, and walked away on tiptoes out of the room. In a few moments, however, she returned with a cup of hot tea. She did not stop asking whether he had any pains, covered him up to his chin, and after Philip signaled to her to remain calm and to not excite the boy even more by her restlessness, she left the room for a while but kept coming back to check upon him. Then Daniel finally fell asleep, exhausted from sobbing for so long.

When he woke up late in the evening, Grandfather Philip sat next to the bed. He drew his chair closer to the bedside and read from one of his sacred books under the light of the kerosene lamp.

"So what? Do you feel better?" he smiled at his grandson from underneath his glasses.

Daniel did not respond. The feverish trembling stopped, but the first glance at Grandfather reminded him of his terrible guilt, and the boy quickly turned his eyes towards the other side.

Philip did not press him further. After a while, he looked up from the book.

"Don't you want to play a game? What about Tick-Tack-Toe? Do you want to?"

But Daniel just shook his head.

After a long time, Philip drew the chair even closer to his grandson's bedside, put the book away, and took the boy's hand into his wrinkled palms.

"Why don't you want to tell me what happened?" he asked suddenly. "Tell me, did anybody hurt you?"

The boy again remained silent, but then all of a sudden, tears welled up in his eyes, and his trembling lips made a desperate admission:

"Nobody hurt me. But I did hurt," he sobbed. "I killed. I killed that comedian who stole Margita from Ivanko. That one who was assaulted by the bull. That was him. I prayed so that God would punish him. I thus killed him."

Slowly, and interrupted by continued sobbing, did the boy's confession exit the gate of his lips, dried-up from fever. Philip felt that Daniel tried to free his hand from Philip's palms several times, but the old man always squeezed it even more tenderly as if he was afraid that he would interrupt Daniel's trust and the flow of his thoughts.

"I killed. Right? I killed him, Grandpa, no?" Daniel again wept bitterly once he confessed everything. He sat on the bed now and pushed his glowing cheeks on Grandfather's hands, which were getting wet from his hot tears. They thus sat for a moment without any movement and without saying a word. Then Philip lifted up the boy's face and put his lips on grandson's forehead.

"You did not kill, my boy. You did not kill him. Stop thinking about it," he talked to him while stroking his black curls. "I like you because you thought about it, but God does not end anybody's life just because somebody else wishes it. Not even to show that he is just. He allows us to either believe in Him or not. Perhaps it was God's punishment. But in that case, God would have punished him even if you had not asked for it. But perhaps it was just some unfortunate coincidence. Nobody will ever know, my boy, whether it was a coincidence or God's punishment. But you have not caused it. Not you."

"Grandpa, you really think that I have not killed him?" Daniel still sniffled.

"No, my boy, for sure not."

Like a healing balm, the old man's words poured on the boy's restless and desperate heart. The splitting headache stopped and was replaced by a sweet weariness that soothed him.

"For sure, Grandpa? He whispered once more.

"For sure. Absolutely sure."

Daniel did not hear anything else. While falling asleep again, he recalled what he had overheard that time behind the door to his grandfather's workshop when Uncle Jacob brought the broken window. How well did he now understand those fragments of Grandfather's sentences that were again sounding in his ears. His heart was not racing somewhere in his throat any more. As if lulled to sleep by the waves of Philip's words echoing in him, Daniel curled up in his warm bed, and his breathing became regular.

Philip covered his grandson even better, then quietly got up, took the book he was reading, and shuffled out of the room without making a sound. At the door, he met Chana, who just wanted to enter the room. With a finger on his lips, he whispered to her:

"He fell asleep. But he feels better. In the morning, he will be fully back to his old self."

"He probably just ate something somewhere," she said under her breath.

"Probably."

"Spitzer is here. He is sitting in the workshop."

Philip passed through the hallway and through the store towards the workshop, where he found his guest. But Spitzer was not sitting on the rocking chair where Chana had seated him. He walked from wall to wall, then shifted from one foot to the other, and it took a while before he shared with Philip why he had truly come. The entire day and the entire night, and even the entire morning today, he had felt on edge. His thoughts were turning around without being able to reach the final decision, like large loaves of bread that were not turning brown despite being baked for a while. He did not gain certainty until this afternoon. He measured the years left in his life as a dough that was kneaded a long time ago but has not yet formed into the shapes of loaves. Then he put on the old broad-brimmed straw hat that usually covered his head in front of God as well as in front of the oven and went for a visit to Aaron Timfeld so that he would reveal to him what he had decided to do as he was the leader of their congregation. Even there, in Rosh Hakol's house, he stood in the same place for a while and shifted from one foot to the other before he removed from his pocket the crumpled bundle of dollar banknotes from his son, a thousand times touched and a thousand times again placed away. He will not go to his son as he cannot leave all that is here. He was born here, lived all his life here, his sons were born here, here he baked the bread, Rosa's grave is here, no, he will not go anywhere else. He thus did not need the money anymore for himself, but perhaps the money could help to save the kehilla. He hoped it was not much less than what Břeclav's Braun would pay, and maybe it was enough for them to survive till the following year when life might get better again. Perhaps they will thus not have to sell the Torah from which his poor Nathan read during a bar mitzvah.

So baker Spitzer decided after torment and endless hours during which he, again and again, pondered all the pros and all the cons and came to share it with Philip Taub now. Philip just quietly listened while his eyes seemed to caress his friend. When the baker finished, he approached him and, without saying a word squeezed his hand.

"Stay with us for dinner tonight. Daniel is in bed and will not eat today. We really have more than enough."

Before he left that evening, Spitzer tiptoed with Philip and Chana to the boy's bedside. Sami will be soon as big as him, Spitzer thought, and for a moment, he felt a heavy weight on his beating heart. He looked again at Daniel, and it occurred to him: He will soon read from the Torah that was saved by me. He and Philip smiled at each other above the bed. Philip then touched his grandson's forehead and said:

"He will be fine tomorrow."

"Tomorrow will be better," Spitzer assured him under his breath while nodding his good-natured oval head.

And tomorrow was better. By the morning, the fever had disappeared, and when at half-past four the shepherd blew the horn at the upper end of the street, Daniel woke up as if he were born again. Only a healthy hunger in an empty stomach reminded him about the bad things from yesterday. He got ready to jump out of bed and to go to the kitchen to cut a slice of bread. But as soon as he moved, a worried Chana woke up as her sleep was very light and forced him to go back to bed, where she covered him under a thick quilt. He tried to assure her in vain that he was feeling well, that he had no pains, and that he really, really did not need anything. He got a cup of tea and a crust of bread but had to stay quiet while resting on the bed.

So he laid down and listened to the sounds of the dawn. The tall entry gates of the houses surrounding the road on both sides squeaked while opening up for cattle passing through them with prolonged lowing. Tomík's cock's imploring crowing was rousing the town from its sleep, and from afar, one could hear the answers from other cocks sounding their bugles. The tone of the shepherd's horn accompanied by the pounding of the flock and the barking of Gipsy, who danced around his new master, was gradually disappearing in the distance.

At six o'clock, the farmers came out to work in the fields and the vineyards. The laughter of women that answered the jokes of well-rested boisterous men mixed in the morning air with the cock crowing.

At seven o'clock, the shuffling steps of Ferenčák resonated through the street. With the postal knapsack over his shoulder, he was delivering mail. Grandfather Philip was already at that time on his way to the synagogue. Under his arm, he carried a velvet bag with the prayerbook and tefillin. And on the corner of Creekside Street, Spitzer already stood waiting for Philip. Ferenčák again waved his hand above his head from a distance, but the baker did not state his usual: "Why is the boy not writing?" He just looked at Philip instead, and they both smiled.

Once they passed through Creekside Street and reached the town square, Philip knocked on the window of the second house from the corner, and in a few moments, they were joined by Gabriel Menasse with the black broad-brimmed hat on his head.

"So you will leave us," was the first thing he said once they exchanged greetings with Spitzer. It again sounded like half a question and half a statement of reality with which they had to become reconciled. But this time, Spitzer did not perceive it as a reproach. He did not reply.

"So we will not walk together for too much longer," Gabriel remarked after a while in the same nagging tone.

But even now, he did not receive any answer. Only behind his back, Philip and the baker grinned at each other.

In the meantime, Chana was still trying to force Daniel back to bed. Below the window, Jura Tomík whistled with his fingers, and Daniel's heart rebelled against the prison underneath the eiderdown. At noontime, Chana allowed him to get up and eat soup at the table, but she could not guard him anymore after lunch. He put on his shirt and trousers, sneaked out of the house, and started to run. He did not stop until he reached the gateway of the yellow house where Grandfather Gabriel lived. At the entrance, he encountered Jacob.

"Uncle Jacob, will you go fishing?" he uttered while still out of breath.

"Not today, my boy. I still have a lot of work."

"It's a pity. I wanted to tell you something."

"What's up?"

Daniel shyly shifted from one foot to the other for a moment but then, before he started to run again, he shouted at Jacob:

"I just wanted to tell you that I like you."

"What?" Jacob shook his head uncomprehendingly.

"That I like you," repeated the boy from the end of the courtyard. He was just jumping up onto the stairs leading to the room where Grandfather Gabriel sat at the window, and Grandmother Theresa sewed something at the table. She looked up at him.

"It is nice that you stopped by to see us," she smiled at her grandson between two stitches. "Wait a moment. I will peel an apple for you." She got up from the table and hobbled to the cupboard on which she kept apples. She peeled off one and handed it to Daniel.

"You are so nice, Grandma, thank you." He sank his teeth into the apple and, while backing out of the room, added: "Grandma, I like you." And at the entrance, while grabbing the door handle, he shouted with his mouth still full: "And you, Grandpa, I like you too."

He ran abruptly out of the room and through the courtyard back to the entrance gateway.

Surprised, Gabriel put his book and pipe away, and together with Theresa, they looked through the window as the boy sped away. Then they smiled at each other, shrugged their shoulders, and before they resumed their reading and sewing, Gabriel laughed out louder than in a long time.

"Meshugge." That was all he said.

What else could he say? What did he know about why Daniel was so full of pity and love for people, so full that he wanted to share it with everybody. With everybody. With everybody from Grandfather Gabriel to old Barbara, from baker Spitzer to Cousin David, and God knows with whom else.

Late in the afternoon, once Philip got back from the mincha prayers, he found the boy in the corner of the room behind the workshop. He was sitting on the floor with his legs crossed and was hugging Dak. The dog wagged his tail joyfully and rubbed Daniel's hand with his head.

"Dak, Dak, I like you," the boy confessed. Philip quietly tiptoed out of the room with a smile on his lips.

At seven o'clock, they gathered at the table. After the dinner, the boy carried four chairs out to the doorstep. Before eight o'clock, Gabriel and Theresa came. Together with Philip and Chana, they sat down on the chairs in front of the house. Daniel, leaning on his mother's lap, watched with them the stars as they were rising in the skies.

"Tomorrow will be a nice day," Philip predicted. Gabriel nodded his head in agreement without removing the pipe out of his mouth.

They just sat and watched the stars.

"So the holidays are coming," Gabriel remarked and puffed out.

"I will send a chicken to the Grün widow," Theresa said after a while.

And they again sat and watched the stars.

"We should also give something to shammash's wife," Chana suggested after a while. "She, nebekh, is again expecting."

"I don't get it. Why that Rév does not take a break," Gabriel grunted but fell silent after Theresa grabbed his sleeve while casting a concerned look at Daniel.

At nine o'clock, Gabriel and Theresa got up.

At ten o'clock, old Ferenčák, armed with his bailiff's saber, dragged a drunken Gipsy from Kohút's pub to the lock-up. Once he double-locked the door behind Gipsy, he removed the sword, hung a bull's horn over his shoulder, and once the conversion from bailiff into night watchman was complete, he got out on a nightly round through the streets.

At midnight, he put the horn to his lips, blew it twelve times, and sang softly while walking slowly to the next corner:

"Twelve o'clock struck,
all souls praise the Lord."

At that time, however, the entire town was already asleep, and nobody listened to his singing. Only Dak stretched out next to Philip's bed, wagging his tail sluggishly in his sleep. And Daniel hugged his quilt even more tightly. He felt at that moment that he was embracing the entire world in his arms.

Epilogue

When he again opened his eyes, he saw that the sun had moved quite far down on its way to the West. He quickly got up and rushed through Creekside Street back to the center of the town. He slowed down only when he had reached the street on which there had to be the one-story yellow house with a store that used to have hanging above its entrance a metal plate with a half-discolored sign:

PHILIP TAUB
GLAZIER AND GROCER

It was not until now that some light began to shine through the thorny shrubs that grew around his heart over so many years – or perhaps it was a wall he himself helped to build around his memories. And it was not until now that he started to fully realize what had changed since the days that passed in front of his eyes up there in the Small Grove. The first glimpse into the world of adults that he recalled was like a pleasant breeze compared to the cruel hurricane that killed and swept away all except him. And why he was saved only God knows.

Awareness of the changes suddenly filled him to the point that he did not experience any disappointment or surprise once he approached the yellow house of his childhood and saw what had been changed there. The store of Grandfather Philip had disappeared and whoever lived there now added a second floor to the building. At the place of the original entrance to the shop, there was a new door reinforced with black iron. For a while, he wondered whether he should enter. For what was he searching there? And could he find what he was searching for? Nothing, nothing was left, everything had changed, everything he will find behind the closed door will be someone else's. And how will he explain why he actually came? For a long time, he stood in front of the gate and could not gather enough courage to push the handle and cross the threshold.

But the gate suddenly opened, and a middle-aged woman wearing a blue apron and with a flowery headscarf walked out with a rolling waddle. It was Kate, their maid. He recognized her, more due to her limping gait rather than her face that had aged considerably. She looked at him for a moment while placing a hand in front of her half-closed near-sighted eyes as if she were dazzled by the sun. Then she moved the hand from her eyes to the front of her mouth as if she were trying to suppress a shout. "Jesus Christ," she called out, "is it possible, or am I just dreaming? Daniel. Daniel came back." She placed on the pavement a basket in which she was carrying something. She then jumped at him and pushed him through the open door into the courtyard, where the dog started to bark.

It took a while before he calmed her down and begged her to not create any unnecessary alarm. He assured her that he had not returned to stay here, that he cannot stay here anymore, that he is just passing through the area and just wanted to briefly stop here and look at the house where he had spent his childhood. He already saw it and will leave soon.

But she did not give up, and when he refused to get inside of the house, she forced him to at least sit down on the bench in the courtyard under the old peach tree, which was still bearing fruit. He was glad to see that something remained unchanged.

Kate dashed off and, in a few minutes, got back with her rolling gait and carried a plate with a blueberry pie. "I myself picked them in the Wet Grove," she told Daniel, and their taste brought back a lot of memories. He ate, and Kate continued to talk. She lives here now with Klvaňas. He is the national committee chairman, and they assigned him the house that was not claimed by anybody, and she, Kate, serves here as a maid. She serves as always. Once she buried her father, Klvaňas took her in to not only serve but to also help with the children as he and his wife were blessed by more of them year by year. Today she had stayed here alone with only the two youngest that were right now sleeping as everybody else had gone to Hodonín for the wedding of the chairman's sister. Kate was content and did not miss anything. Long ago, she had reconciled with the fact that she would not have her own family, but she at least took care of the children of others and loved them as if they were her own. They gave her a small room, that one where Mr. Philip used to sit and read his sacred books. Kate thought about the old man and about Daniel's mother quite often.

"Nobody came back," she repeated again and again. "Nobody came back." Daniel knew. He knew that he was the last one to be called to the altar to read for the first time from the Torah. He also knew that Spitzer's son had come here and taken the old baker to America with him. But he also knew that he had died there in not more than a year. It was, he recalled, just before they had gathered all of them at the town square and then took them to the railway station on the journey that turned out to be the last one for everybody else.

"Nobody came back," she repeated, and Daniel knew that he was the only one left so that somebody could recite the prayer kaddish for the entire congregation.

And Kate shared with him what was stolen by the new lords and what was removed from the empty houses by others. "Nothing. Nothing was left. And whatever might be still left was for sure after so many years just some wreckage and some shreds."

She then ran away again to check whether the children did not wake up. Daniel used this moment of solitude to look around the courtyard. In the meantime, the dog calmed down, laid stretched out in front of the doghouse, and did not growl when Daniel passed around to the woodshed. At the place where Grandfather Philip used to store sheets of glass, there was something shiny in the dust. He bent over and picked up a chip of colored glass.

Perhaps it was that chip that they had placed on their bare feet when they played heaven-inferno-paradise. Maybe it had waited all that time here for him, thought Daniel, and hid the fragment of glass whose edges were smoothed by time into his pocket.

He did not want anything else other than this chip of glass. However, when Kate returned, she took something out of her apron and handed it to him. A small case, either from the silver or at least silver-plated, in the shape of a boat. He immediately recognized it. Grandfather Philip used to keep in it grains of aromatic spices whose fragrance elevated the holy Shabbat over the dullness of the weekdays. He took a sniff at it, and it seemed to him that even now, the scent of the Shabbats from the distant past did not waft away. His heart started to beat when he heard: "Nothing was left. I saved only this. It is yours now, my dear Daniel." She talked to him as if he was still a small boy, and he felt at that moment better than in so many years. He could not even thank her enough. He just grasped the boat in his palms and again and again tried to smell the long-forgotten fragrance.

But the time to leave had come. They overheard a baby crying, and she had to check on the children. Daniel thus parted without spending too much time saying goodbye. The fragment of glass that he had used for playing heaven-inferno-paradise, and the case in the shape of the boat with the fragrance of childhood, was all he was taking away with him.

He rushed to the railway station. He did not even turn around to look back. It was late afternoon, and as he passed through the streets, he met many people, but nobody recognized him. Once in a while, somebody glanced at his face with curiosity, but nobody greeted him. He thought that he knew some of the passers-by, but even he himself was not entirely sure and was not in the mood to initiate any conversations now. He was not in the mood, but he also did not have enough time as it was late, and he could not afford to miss the train that would take him away from here. And it was the last train of that day.

When he got to the railway station, he learned that the train was delayed. The waiting room was full of men and countrywomen with bags. It was smoky there, and the scent of cheap cigarettes, soot, and sweat mixed with the pungent odor of urine penetrating through the wet wall. He thus quickly got out and sat on the bench at the platform. Even in front of the building, he could smell the oil and the steam, but near the station, locust trees were blooming, and the soft evening breeze brought their sweet fragrance up to here.

In that aroma, everything was growing sweeter – even his memories. For a moment, he wanted to, for a moment, he was even able to forget about everything that happened later, and he again became a small boy trembling with fear from the first glimpse into the world of adults. And for a moment, they all disappeared, and only Grandfather Philip was left with him. He was again soothing him like before: "Nobody will ever know what is a coincidence and what is God's punishment."

And then he suddenly also saw Uncle Jacob. He came to Grandfather with the broken window, and Grandfather spoke to him like before: "God? I believe that He is just but also full of mercy. I believe but will never know for sure whether He exists or not. And we really need to acknowledge that. We are pitiful, we all are pitiful, we are like children in a dark forest. And perhaps because of that, we have to be nice, we have to hold our hands in the darkness, we have to be full of pity for others."

He remembered everything Grandfather said. He did not forget a word. "Pity, pity, pity for others." But those others were murders. They killed Grandfather Philip, they killed Uncle Jacob, they killed everybody, everybody else.

Grandfather Philip felt pity for them, but they killed even him. Pity did not seem to help. But he still heard Grandfather repeating that same word again and again: "Pity, pity, pity. There is nothing stronger in our life, nothing more beautiful, nothing better."

"A pity for murders?" he asked and could not reconcile with that thought.

But Grandfather replied: "Even for them. Even they are children in the darkness. Even they are pitiful. Perhaps even more pitiful than us."

"More pitiful than their innocent victims? More pitiful than the dead?" he continued to ask, but Grandfather disappeared without any answer, and Daniel only knew that there were more things he would never know for sure.

Suddenly everybody streamed out of the waiting room to the platform, and the coarse voices of the men and the high-pitched shouting of mothers calling up their children interrupted his daydreaming. He saw that Jura Tomík, in the uniform of a dispatcher, was already in front of them and was pushing them away from the rails as the train drawn by the puffing and blowing steam engine was approaching.

The train stopped, and they all rushed through the released steam to the stairs on the train cars. He did not know how he joined the crowd, but they were all shoving him with their bodies and bags till they pushed him into one compartment where he sat down on the bench next to the window from which one could see the platform with the inner wall of the station. He once more caught a glimpse of dispatcher Tomík. Perhaps he should have disclosed his identity to him. But it was too late now. He lifted up the sign and let the engine driver know that the rails were clear. The engine inhaled like a weight lifter, then it exhaled twice, and the train slowly started to move.

Despite sitting at the window, Daniel did not look at the town as it was passing around him. He was even unsure whether he had chosen to board this train that was taking him away or whether he was seated there by the wish of somebody he did not know. He only knew that he would never know for sure.

He put his hands in his coat pockets and touched the glass fragment and the small boat with the grains of aromatic spices. He rolled the chip smoothed by time between his fingers for a while until he felt its hidden warmth. Then he secretly removed the small case from the pocket, hid it in his cupped hand, and took a sniff at it. The Shabbat fragrance of the spices did not waft away. And it will never pass away, he said to himself.

That was all he took with him. Yet, suddenly he felt that it was more than enough.

Glossary

In place of footnotes to better understand this novel, selected Yiddish, Hebrew, and Czech words and phrases are listed here in alphabetical order.

Aliyah shlishi – aliyah is the calling of a member of the congregation to recite the blessing before and after a section of the Torah is read; during Shabbat services, there are seven sections, and shlishi is the third one.

Bar Mitzvah – Jewish coming of age ritual for boys during which they read from the Torah for the first time in front of the congregation, and are counted for the ritual quorum.

Barches – also called Challah, braided bread traditionally eaten during Shabbat dinners and on other holidays.

Besamim – spices in Hebrew, usually refers to the container with aromatic spices used during Shabbat rituals and blessings.

Git Shabes – Yiddish for "Good Shabbos" or "Shabbat Shalom".

Goy – a non-Jewish man, from a Yiddish dialect.

Goyte – a non-Jewish woman, a female version of goy, from a Yiddish dialect.

Heaven-inferno-paradise – game resembling hopscotch.

Kaddish – an ancient prayer recited for the dead.

Kehilla – means congregation or assembly in Hebrew, the word was used for Jewish communal structures in Eastern Europe.

Kittel – from Yiddish, a white robe or shroud worn on holidays, it is also often used during burials, reflects the words from Isaiah 1:18, "our sins shall be made as white as snow".

Kreuzer – a copper coin used in the Austrian empire.

Leshana tova tikateivu – means "be inscribed for a good year (in the Book of Life)" in Hebrew, a formal greeting exchanged on Rosh Hashanah.

Mariáš – a three-player Czech card game; the name is a phonetic transcription of the French "mariage".

Mazal tov – "good fortune" in Hebrew, the phrase used to express congratulations on important life events such as a wedding or childbirth.

Menorah – a seven branch candelabrum

Menuche – from Hebrew menucha, which means rest, calm, or serenity.

Meshugge – crazy, from Yiddish.

Mincha – afternoon prayer service, from Hebrew.

Mizrach – the Hebrew word for "East", it refers to the ornament usually decorated with lions of Judah holding the Decalogue hung on the east wall of a synagogue or a house in the direction of Jerusalem towards which Jews face when in prayer.

Mohel – a person who performs ritual circumcisions, from Hebrew.

Nebbish – a weak or inept person and regarded as pitifully ineffectual, usually used with disdain, from Yiddish.

Nebekh – unfortunately or "such a pity", from Yiddish.

Ner Tamid – eternal light in Hebrew, it hangs above the Ark in every synagogue, as a reminder of the eternal flame that burned on the altar of the Temple in Jerusalem.

Pesach (Passover) – Holiday celebrating the liberation of Israel from captivity in Egypt in the time of Moses.

Rebbe – Yiddish variant of Hebrew word rabbi which means master or teacher.

Revoch – profit, from Yiddish and Hebrew.

Rimonim – ornaments used to decorate the Torah scroll, they are usually made of silver, with gemstones and bells hanging off the sides.

Rosh Hakol – in Hebrew head or chief of all, the term was used for the head or president of the Jewish community in Eastern Europe.

Rosh Hashanah – the Jewish New Year, celebrated on the first day of the month Tishri (usually in September).

Sandek – the man honored with holding the baby during the Jewish circumcision ceremony.

Seder – ceremonial dinner at the start of Passover.

Shammash – Hebrew word for servant, used for synagogue attendants and helpers who assist the cantor and rabbi.

Shana Tovah – means "Good Year" in Hebrew, is used as a traditional New Year greeting and wish during the Rosh Hashanah holiday.

Shiva – Hebrew word for seven, used for mourning rituals for the immediate family of the deceased as the mourning period lasts seven days; participation in those rituals is referred to as "to sit shiva".

Shofar – a ritual musical instrument usually made from the horn of a ram, used during important religious celebrations like Rosh Hashanah and Yom Kippur.

Shul – Yiddish for synagogue.

Sma 'Jisroel – from Hebrew "Sh'ma Yisrael" which means "Hear, O Israel"; those are the first two words of the most important Jewish prayer, the full text is "Hear, O Israel: The Lord our God, the Lord is one" (Deuteronomy 6:4).

Tallit – a garment, traditionally worn as a prayer shawl; it has special twined and knotted fringes known as tzitzit, attached to its four corners.

Tas – metal shield covering for the Torah, often in the shape of a plaque topped with a crown and decorated with Jewish symbols, usually made from a wrought silver.

Tefillin – a pair of black small leather boxes with straps containing scrolls inscribed with verses from the Torah, the set includes two boxes – one is strapped to the head and one to the arm.

Tishri – the Hebrew month of the Jewish year when the Jewish high holidays are observed, coincides with September or October.

Torah – the Law of God, recorded in the five books of Moses and inscribed on the scroll.

Treif – Yiddish word for non-kosher or not permitted food; the word is derived from Hebrew terefah.

Tzimmes – a sweet Jewish food made from pears, cabbage, and carrots with sugar and honey, usually eaten only during the celebration of Rosh Hashanah.

Tzitzit – ritual fringes attached to each corner of a four-cornered garment.

Yad – literally "hand" in Hebrew, a ritual pointer used by the Torah reader to follow the text as the Torah is read aloud, it is usually made from silver and is typically shaped like a long rod capped by a small hand.

Yasher Koach – means "may you have strength" in Hebrew; used as an expression of congratulations to those who were honored with an aliyah to Torah.

Yevarechecha – means "God bless" in Hebrew, it is part of the text of the priestly blessing, said by the Kohen, sometimes said by the rabbi to his congregation or by the father to his children.

Yom Kippur – also known as the Day of Atonement, it is the holiest day of the Jewish year, characterized by a day-long fast and intensive prayers, observed on the 10th of Tishri.

Made in the USA
Columbia, SC
04 October 2023

23910804R00112